CLEMENTINE
FLORENTINE

CLEMENTINE FLORENTINE

WRITTEN BY
TASHA HARRISON

ILLUSTRATED BY
MYA MITCHELL

uclanpublishing

HAVE YOU EVER WONDERED HOW BOOKS ARE MADE?

UCLan Publishing is an award winning independent publisher specialising in Children's and Young Adult books. Based at The University of Central Lancashire, this Preston-based publisher teaches MA Publishing students how to become industry professionals using the content and resources from its business; students are included at every stage of the publishing process and credited for the work that they contribute.

The business doesn't just help publishing students though. UCLan Publishing has supported the employability and real-life work skills for the University's Illustration, Acting, Translation, Animation, Photography, Film & TV students and many more. This is the beauty of books and stories; they fuel many other creative industries! The MA Publishing students are able to get involved from day one with the business and they acquire a behind the scenes experience of what it is like to work for a such a reputable independent.

The MA course was awarded a Times Higher Award (2018) for Innovation in the Arts and the business, UCLan Publishing, was awarded Best Newcomer at the Independent Publishing Guild (2019) for the ethos of teaching publishing using a commercial publishing house. As the business continues to grow, so too does the student experience upon entering this dynamic Masters course.

www.uclanpublishing.com
www.uclanpublishing.com/courses/
uclanpublishing@uclan.ac.uk

Clementine Florentine is a uclanpublishing book

First published in Great Britain in 2022 by
uclanpublishing
University of Central Lancashire
Preston, PR1 2HE, UK

978-1-912979-71-4

13 5 7 9 10 8 6 4 2

Set in 10/18pt Pembroke by Becky Chilcott.

A CIP catalogue record for this book is available from the British Library.

Printed and bound in Great Britain by Clays Ltd, Elcograf S.p.A.

To anyone who thinks they're
'not good enough' . . .
You *are*.

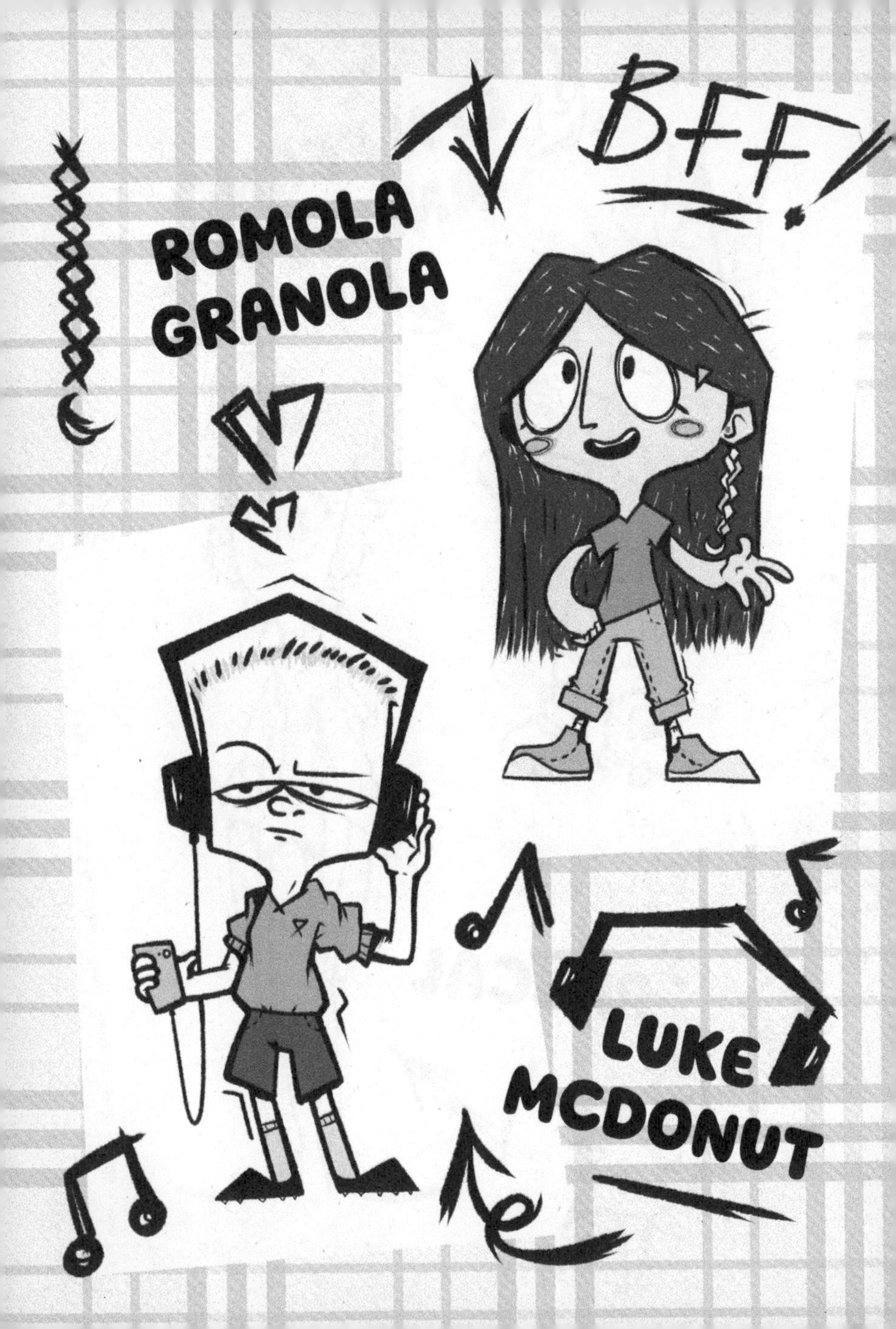
BFF!
ROMOLA GRANOLA
LUKE MCDONUT

INGRID PARTRIDGE

EDDIE TWO-BALLS

CHAPTER 1

SATURDAY 1ST SEPTEMBER

THERE WAS NO DOUBT ABOUT IT — MY DAD WAS ACTING STRANGELY.

Two days ago, he'd walked into the kitchen and trodden in a poo left by Fred, our old and confused cat. Normally Dad would've done his nut but this time, he didn't. Instead, an hour or so later, I'd heard him on his phone, laughing his head off about it.

Most out of character.

Then yesterday he'd cleaned the shower doors (for the first time ever), vacuumed under the sofas (extremely rare) and bought some new cushions 'to brighten up the

front room'. (Neon yellow. Since when did Dad buy *neon yellow*?)

Today, he was dusting my bedroom and singing (rather than working on his blog and grumbling). And Lottie and I had been given jobs to do.

'Is the Queen coming for tea or something?' I asked as he ran the feather duster along my bookshelves.

'Just having a spring clean, Clem-cakes, that's all.'

'But it's almost autumn.'

'Well, it's way overdue. When I picked you guys up from Mum's flat yesterday, she said it's high time you kids took on more responsibilities – and I totally agree. Check this out!' I looked up from grooming Fred as Dad extended his fingertip to reveal a small mound of grey fluff. 'That's just from *one* picture frame.'

'Gross. Check *this* out!' I held up the cat brush rammed with fur.

'Good job. He looks healthier already.'

I doubted that. Fred was on a strict diet – vet's orders. As I plucked the fur from the brush, he escaped and thundered downstairs.

Lottie wandered into my room wearing her camo combat shorts and matching cap and aimed her bow and arrow at

Dad. 'Can I leave cleaning Mr Miyagi's tank till tomorrow?' she asked, firing the plastic arrow at his chest.

'Not if you don't want me to report you to the RSPCA for cruelty to goldfish or cancel your taekwondo lessons with immediate effect.' He tugged her scruffy French plait. 'And tidy up your weaponry, too, while you're at it.'

'OKAAY!' huffed my little sister, picking up her arrow and stomping downstairs.

'Wrong direction!' Dad shouted.

'I'm getting the jug to put Mr Miyagi in!' she shouted back.

'Right, what's next on my list?' Dad stroked his stubbly chin and thought to himself. 'Ah, yes – clean inside the fridge. By the way, can you open your window? Your room smells like a fart that's been trapped in a bottle for a thousand years.' He closed my door behind him.

RUDE! And super-hypocritical coming from The Fart Lord himself. I sniffed the air. My room smelt fine, thank you very much.

I took my poem book out of my desk drawer and stroked its marbled cover.

It was time.

Time for *Clementine Florentine* to start writing poems again.

It felt like ages since I'd last used my pen name. Clementine Florentine was the nickname my parents called me when I was a baby – and still called me to this day. Having a pen name helped me feel like a poet and, as a poem had been brewing in my head since we took Fred to the vet's last week, I couldn't ignore it any longer. No one was going to see it anyway, so what did it matter if it wasn't very good?

This was the first poem I'd felt like writing since I'd entered the Ferndale Juniors Poetry Challenge at the end of last term – and lost. I'd thought my poem about custard creams was really good and I was certain I was going to win, but I wasn't even a runner-up. And, as if I didn't feel disappointed enough, the winner – who'd only joined our school two weeks before (SO unfair) – had made a snarky remark about my poem that had echoed in my ears almost every day since.

'*Call that a poem? That's rubbish! No wonder yours didn't win.*' I took a deep breath. So what if I wasn't the best poet in the world? I enjoyed it and that's what mattered. I probably wouldn't enter any more competitions from now on, but when a poem started forming in my head, it needed to come out.

Clementine Florentine needed to come out.

So, I pressed my biro against the page and began.

POOR FRED

We fed you too much and you've put on weight
But our super-strict vet says it's not too late
You need to be healthy and fit through your flap
And live a long life till you're a very old cat

I was trying to think of what rhymed with kilos (smaller meal-os?) when Lottie yelled from the kitchen.

'Look! Look! Ingrid's got a new costume!'

I hurried downstairs to the kitchen where my sister was perched on top of the sofa pointing out the window at our neighbour Ingrid, who had also been our teacher in reception.

Dad arrived behind me and opened the window that looked on to the street. Ingrid, who lives in the flat opposite our house, was standing on her doorstep in a full-length, white, flowing dress with a gold sash round the middle, a shield in one hand and a sword in the other, her long brown hair flapping like a flag in the wind. Eddie Two-Balls, her chocolate Springador, was sitting next to her; a centurion's

6

helmet on his head and two tennis balls squished, as usual, between his jaws.

'You're a goddess!' shouted Lottie.

'I'm Athena, goddess of WAR, baby!' Ingrid gestured to the floaty material with her sword. 'Guess how much?'

'Fifty pence' shouted Lottie. Ingrid shook her head.

'Seven pounds fifty!' I shouted.

Ingrid pointed her sword at me. 'Correctomondo, Clementine. Bargain, eh?'

'So, are you teaching Greek gods in reception next term?' asked Dad.

'Nah,' said Ingrid. 'Just another charity shop find – couldn't resist.'

'I like it even more than your Sleeping Beauty dress,' said Lottie.

'Thanks, babes. Laters!' Ingrid waved goodbye and went inside.

'Completely bonkers that one, bless her,' said Dad, closing the window.

'She's *not* bonkers,' protested Lottie. 'She's really, *really* nice. She was my favourite teacher in the infants.'

'Yeah, you're mean,' I said, agreeing with my sister for once.

'I'm *not* mean!' Dad looked offended. 'Ingrid is lovely,

just a little . . . nuts.'

'Enjoying dressing up in fun outfits doesn't make you nuts, it makes you FUN!' scowled Lottie, taking the glass jug from the draining board.

Dad laughed. 'All right, Captain Foghorn. Point taken.'

'Yeah, listen to my wiseyness.' Lottie gave a self-righteous nod, tucked the jug under her armpit and scampered back upstairs.

Dad's phone started ringing. He looked at the screen, smiled and answered it. 'Just a sec, Mel.' He held it away from his ear. 'Tell Lottie tea will be ready in an hour, Clem.' He nodded towards the kitchen door – a signal to give him some privacy.

Who was this Mel? He was on the phone to her the other day, too. I would've sat on the stairs earwigging, but my own phone beeped so I went into my room to see who'd messaged me. It was Rom, back from a big family reunion in Italy – *finally!*

Rom: Helloooo, I'm back!

Me: YAY! Can I come next time?!
The swimming pool looked amazing.

Rom: Yeah, but with all my rellies in it,
there was no room to swim!
Anything happen while I was away?

Me: If only. Fred's on a diet, my dad's acting
weird and my sister keeps attacking me with her
bow & arrows. (She saw a clip of *The Hunger
Games* and wants to be a freedom fighter).
I'm SO glad you're back!

Rom: Well, only 38 hours 34 minutes till
we're in Mr C's class!!! 🦉 🦉 🦉
Walk to school together Monday morning?

Me: YOU BET!
Meet by corner shop at 8.30.
Year 6 here we come! Wooooo!

I lay on my bed and decided to start making a list of
everything that rhymed with kilos at the back of my poem
book. A guffaw of laughter boomed up the stairs. Dad was
obviously still on the phone to Mel, cooking our tea with
one hand. I opened my door to eavesdrop.

'I'm putting you on speaker,' said Dad. 'No, it's fine, they're both upstairs.'

A woman's voice echoed out of Dad's phone. 'So, I've been reading your blog . . .'

'*Seriously?* I've only got one follower – my neighbour, Ingrid.'

There was a loud, screechy, snorty laugh that sounded like a cross between a witch's cackle and a horse neighing. 'Well, now you've got *two* followers. I love how you talk about music with a sense of humour – and I'm going to buy that album you just reviewed.'

'*Really?*' Dad sounded super-chuffed. The noise of the kettle boiling drowned out their voices and I closed my bedroom door, feeling slightly uneasy.

Whoever Mel was, Dad clearly liked her a lot because he never usually laughed that much when talking to people on the phone. And although hearing him laugh was a good thing, why did I feel a bit weird about it? I pushed the feeling away and returned to my list. Kilo was an annoyingly unrhymey word.

'Clem-cakes! Foghorn! Tea's ready!' Dad's voice sailed up the stairs and we emerged from our rooms and trooped down to the kitchen.

'Is it bangers and mash?' I asked hopefully. I was craving mashed potato.

'Macaroni cheese,' Dad replied with a strange grin on his face. I sighed.

As he dolloped it on to our plates, Lottie narrowed her eyes at him. 'Why are you grinning?'

I looked at Dad. He was so busy smiling he didn't even hear her.

'DAD!' shouted Lottie, making him jump. 'ARE YOU ON PLANET MERMICORN?'

'For goodness' sake, Lottie! Do you always have to shout?' snapped Dad.

'What were you thinking about?' asked Lottie.

'I was wondering what to cook for Sunday lunch tomorrow, as it looks like we'll be having guests.'

'Who?' we chorused.

'My new friend, Mel,' Dad beamed. 'And she's bringing her son who, it turns out, Clem already knows. His name's Callum – joined Ferndale Juniors at the end of last term.'

'*Callum Harvey?*' I froze, my fork halfway to my mouth.

'That's right! And, as if that wasn't coincidence enough,' said Dad excitedly, 'I found out when I was talking to Mel

just now that Callum's a bit of a poet too. Did you know you had that in common, Clem?'

Those sneering words rang in my ears yet again: '*Call that a poem? That's rubbish! No wonder yours didn't win.*'

'Clem? Are you OK?' Dad frowned at me. 'You've gone all red.'

I put down my knife and fork. 'Callum Harvey is a TOTAL MORON!' I blurted. 'I one hundred per cent HATE him. You've got to cancel lunch tomorrow – PLEASE!'

They both stared at me like I was mad.

'Why do you hate Callum?' asked Dad. 'What did he do?'

'He said my poem was rubbish.'

Lottie rolled her eyes. 'Seriously, *is that all*?'

Fuming, I got up, yanked Lottie's plait as hard as I could, and stormed upstairs.

CHAPTER 2

TWENTY MINUTES LATER

I'D BEEN IN MY ROOM SULKING FOR WHAT FELT LIKE AGES, WHEN FINALLY THERE WAS A KNOCK ON MY BEDROOM DOOR.

I waited for Dad to read my sign – he'd soon get the message.

I was lying face down on my bed, with Bob, my cuddly monkey, trapped beneath me. I'd thrown Bob across the room in a fit of rage, picked him up and apologised, then, for the first time in years, wrapped his dangly arms around me for a much-needed hug.

'Can I come in?' he said from the other side of my door.

'READ THE SIGN!' I shouted.

'Which one? Your door is *covered* in signs!' There was a pause. 'Wait, the one entitled 'Updated Instructions for Entering Clementine's Room'?'

Duh, obviously.

Dad cleared his throat. '1. Knock. 2. Wait for Clementine to answer door. 3. If door is not answered, Clementine is either out or in a bad mood so GO AWAY.'

The handle turned and the door opened.

DISRESPECTFUL!

'We need to talk, Clem.' Dad came and sat on the edge of my bed. 'Why didn't you tell me what Callum said about your poem at the time?'

'You were busy.'

'I'm never too busy to listen to my daughter when she's upset.'

'But *you* were upset yourself.'

Dad scratched his short grey hair. 'I was? Remind me.'

'Your boss didn't like your new ideas for the newsletter. And you were worried she didn't like you working from home any more. And you were miserable cos no one ever reads your blog.'

Dad nodded. 'Ah yes, I remember. Sometimes I get a bit

frustrated with life, but you don't need to worry about me, Clem, I promise. My problems are small fry compared to my kids' happiness. I'm here for you, night and day, no matter what's going on in my life. Never feel like you can't come to me.'

I sat up and propped Bob up on the bed between me and Dad. 'Yeah, but Lottie's kind of right. Someone saying my poem's rubbish isn't a big deal.'

'It *is* when poetry's your *thing*! No wonder I haven't seen any new poems over the summer – sounds like he knocked your confidence.' Dad tilted my face towards him. 'Listen to me, Clem. You're a *great* poet, and you *love* writing poems. Never let anyone take that away from you. You're *Clementine Florentine*, remember? Do you know how proud me and Mum are of you?'

Dad enveloped me in a hug, squashing Bob between us.

'In fact, let me take a picture of you and Bob to send to Mum. It'll cheer her up while she's in Hong Kong.' Dad took his phone out of his pocket and pointed it at me. I tried to smile. *Click*.

'When's she back?' I asked.

'Two weeks today. And you're spending that weekend with her.'

Mum travelled a lot for work, so we didn't have a set routine like most other split families did.

'So, are you going to cancel lunch tomorrow?' I asked, as he tucked my unbrushed hair behind my ear.

He sighed. 'I can't, Clem. It would be rude to invite someone then uninvite them a few hours later.'

I turned my face away.

'Look, I'm not making excuses for Callum – he shouldn't have said that about your poem – but bear in mind that, in the last year, his parents have split up, he's moved from London to Brighton and joined a new school at the end of Year Five where everyone else has known each other since reception. Maybe Callum was being cocky because he was trying to act more confidently than he actually felt.'

I huffed. 'Well if he acted NICE instead of cocky, he'd make friends a lot quicker.'

'I agree,' said Dad. 'But feeling insecure can make us act in silly ways. I bet you he regrets what he said. Can you give him a second chance? If he's mean to you again, then I'll have a word with Mel – or Mr C, if you'd prefer?'

'DON'T TALK TO MR C!' I pounced on Dad, pinning him to the bed. 'Swear you won't talk to Mr C!'

I didn't want to start Year Six with Mr C thinking I was a precious princess whose over-protective dad stepped in whenever someone called my poem rubbish.

'OK, OK!' spluttered Dad. 'Get off, Clem – you're hurting me. I swear I won't talk to the *legend* that is Mr C.'

I backed off.

'I don't get why he's such a *legend* though? Is it because he's got a bit of a pop star vibe going on?'

I rolled my eyes. 'No, it's because he's the most unteachery teacher at Ferndale Juniors.'

'Just tell me if Callum's mean to you again, OK? Because I think Mel would want to know. Like you say, he won't be doing himself any favours going around being cocky and rude to people.'

'Is Mel your girlfriend?' I asked.

Dad looked a bit startled. Then his eyes drifted into the distance. He was back on Planet Mermicorn, as Lottie would say.

'No. Well, not yet. It's early days, Clem – that's why I haven't mentioned her before now. I'm still getting to know her. For now, we're just friends. If our friendship develops into something more . . . I'll let you know.'

'How did you meet her?'

17

'I met her in a bookshop. We were in the queue for the till and started chatting when we noticed we were both buying the same book. Then, a week later, I bumped into her in the pub and invited her out for coffee.' Dad stood up. 'So, are we OK about tomorrow?'

I sighed. 'Suppose so.'

'I really appreciate it. Thank you.' He turned towards the door and sniffed. 'You never opened the window in here, did you?'

'My room does NOT smell!' I sniffed the air. Or did it?

'Trust me, it does.' Dad marched over to the window and yanked up the sash pane. 'Why don't you come downstairs and finish your macaroni? Give me a few minutes and I'll heat it up in the microwave.'

I got up and put Bob back on my bookcase with my other cuddly toys.

'Haven't seen you cuddling Bob Monkhouse in years,' laughed Dad as he went downstairs.

'It's just Bob – *not* Bob Monkhouse,' I reminded him for the millionth time.

I belly-flopped on to my bed, stared hard at my 'Poor Fred' poem, and suddenly it came to me. Not *kilos* but . . .

No more naughty treats, and no more ham
You need to lose three thousand grams
So stop whining for food my greedy little pet
Or we'll all be in trouble with our super-strict vet

A noise made me look up from my poem. My sister had better not be planning an attack. I lay very still and listened. There it was again – a fluttery, purry sound, followed by a *tap, scratch, tap, scratch*. It couldn't be Lottie – she would've invaded by now. And it wasn't Fred, because I'd heard him go out through the cat flap with a loud clatter a few minutes ago.

Something wasn't right.

I stood up, closed my window and looked around my room, turning slowly in a circle. My hedgehog collection wasn't missing any hedgehogs. (A few had made their way into Lottie's room over the years 'of their own free will' apparently). My Lego dream house (designed and built by myself) still had a layer of dust on it that Dad had missed. My Little Mix poster was still wonky. My bin was overflowing (I was supposed to empty it after grooming Fred – *oops*). My bookcase had all my Gallagher Girls books, my bowl of hair accessories, my tub of slime, my family of cuddly toys including Olaf, Manny from *Ice Age*, Maximus Bear, Minimus Bear, Micromus Bear, Lemmy the lion, Jemima the giraffe, Bob and Parrot.

WAIT! WHAT?

SINCE WHEN DID I HAVE A PARROT?

I did a double take.

An actual living, breathing, three-dimensional, multi-coloured parrot was perched on the end of my bookshelves like a bookend, looking at me with beady eyes. It opened its red, blue and yellow wings, squawked loudly and folded them again.

'*O. M. ACTUAL G*,' I gasped, my pen and poem book sliding from my hands. 'What the bonkers conkers from Honkers is an *actual live parrot* doing on my shelves?'

The parrot scratched itself with a leathery claw and let out another almighty screech.

I quickly shut my door. I needed some space and privacy while I figured out what to do.

'Where did you come from?' I whispered.

'*Bing bong!*' sang the parrot. '*Bing bong! Bing bong! Bing bong! SQUAWK!*'

It shuffled from one foot to the other, curling its claws round the wooden rail of my bookcase.

'Do you belong to someone?' I whispered. 'Or did you escape from the zoo? Or did you fly all the way here from the Amazon rainforest?' I checked the parrot's legs for tags but there were no clues at all as to where it had come from.

I looked at the parrot. She – or he – looked back at me.

'Punk is dead!' she chirped.

'What?'

'Punk is dead! *Bing bong! SQUAWK!*'

I giggled. 'You're so funny! Who *are* you? What are you doing in *my* bedroom? You're totally welcome to stay for as long as you like – for ever, even!'

Was this some kind of sign? Was I . . . *The Chosen One* – chosen to look after this amazing, beautiful bird? Imagine that! Me, the proud owner of a *pet parrot*?

'Clem!' Dad yelled from downstairs. 'Your macaroni's ready!'

'Dad can't know about you,' I whispered to the parrot. 'There's *no way* he'd let you stay, and I can't give you back just yet because you only just got here and I *so* want you to stay for a while. So, *shhhhh!*'

I pressed my finger to my lips and tiptoed backwards out of my room, closing the door gently behind me.

CHAPTER 3

THE FOLLOWING MORNING

THE FIRST THING I DID THIS MORNING, AFTER CHECKING ON PERRIE (THE NAME CAME TO ME AS I WAS FALLING ASLEEP LAST NIGHT STARING AT MY LITTLE MIX POSTER) AND WOLFING DOWN SOME TOAST, WAS TO MAKE A NEW EXTRA-BOLD SIGN AND STICK IT ON MY BEDROOM DOOR:

AMENDED INSTRUCTIONS
FOR ENTERING
CLEMENTINE'S ROOM:

1. KNOCK.

2. WAIT FOR CLEMENTINE TO ANSWER DOOR

3. IF DOOR ISN'T ANSWERED,
GO AWAY. DO NOT ENTER UNDER
ANY CIRCUMSTANCES. DO NOT
OPEN DOOR – NOT EVEN A BIT.

4. DO NOT DEFY ME.

The next thing I did was to FaceTime Rom.

'Are you alone?' I asked. 'I've got something to show you – but it's a secret.'

Rom looked over her shoulder to check her parents and older sister weren't hovering nearby. 'The coast is clear,' she reported, her brown eyes twinkling.

'Look!' I turned the camera towards Perrie and listened to Rom squeal with excitement. '*Ssh!*' I giggled. 'No one can know – *especially not my dad*.'

I showed her Perrie's bowl of muesli, water and toilet station (some newspaper spread out on the floor at the foot of my bookcase) and told her what I'd learnt from googling

24

'types of parrots' – that Perrie was a scarlet macaw with the intelligence of an eight-year-old child. (The same age as my sister!)

'But Clem,' Rom said when she'd eventually calmed down, 'what if Perrie's owner is desperate to find her?'

I sighed. It had already occurred to me that Perrie's owner might be freaking out. But then, they should've taken better care of her, shouldn't they?

'Maybe Perrie escaped from someone who treated her badly?' I said.

'Maybe,' said Rom. 'You should probably call the RSPB. They'll know what to do. If they think Perrie wasn't being looked after properly, then they might let you keep her?'

Rom was probably right. She'd done a lot of research on rare birds for her art project last term. She'd made a series of colourful information posters on different types of birds, followed by a giant bird of paradise piñata that Mrs Barraclough held up in assembly, making everyone go 'Wow!' before hanging it in the school library. Because of the piñata, everyone at school knew who Rom was and thought she was super cool. But I knew her better than anyone and if anything, she was more super sensible than super cool. Dad would joke that while Rom liked making things, I liked making trouble. And then he'd apologise and say he was only joking and that my poems were every bit as brilliant as Rom's artistic creations.

'Hey, Clem, want to come over and do some baking later?' she asked. 'I want to try making a rainbow cake, but with *seven* colours instead of five.' (Rom also loved a challenge – especially when it came to baking).

'I can't,' I said, gutted. I loved being Rom's assistant bowl-licker. 'We've got guests coming for lunch. You'll never guess who,' I said, in my voice of doom. 'Callum *butt-face* Harvey and his mum.'

'WHAT?' Rom's shocked face filled my phone screen.

'I know,' I said.

'Maybe he'll apologise for being mean about your poem?' said Rom.

'Doubt it.'

'Why are him and his mum coming for lunch?'

I was going to explain but Perrie started squawking. 'I'll tell you tomorrow,' I said, shushing Perrie and stroking her feathers.

'Good luck,' she said. 'And don't forget to call the RSPB!'

Even though Rom was right about reporting Perrie missing, I couldn't bring myself to part with her just yet.

I was still trying to figure out what to do a few hours later when the doorbell rang.

The Dreaded Duo were here.

My heart started beating faster. I could not let Callum Harvey make me feel nervous and wobbly in my own home.

Voices wafted upstairs from the hallway.

Lottie skipped past my bedroom door and bounded downstairs. I checked my reflection in the mirror: I was wearing my fingerless gloves, checked beret and sort-of-matching waistcoat, baggy ripped jeans and fluorescent green socks. Dad called it my Shermadge outfit (short for Sherlock Holmes-meets-Madonna). To my horror, my cheeks were bright red. This was clearly my body's way of protesting at the stress I was about to endure. I flapped at my cheeks, willing them to cool down and return to their usual, pale blotchiness.

'Clem!' Dad called out. 'Our guests are here!'

I pulled a vomit face. 'Coming!'

'You've got to be really quiet,' I whispered, stroking Perrie's head.

'*Bing bong!*' said Perrie.

'No bing bongs,' I said.

'*Bing bong! Bing bong! SQUAWK!*'

'*Sssssh*, Perrie, please!' I edged out of my room. 'I'll check on you later.'

'Punk is dead!'

I closed the door behind me and slowly padded downstairs to the kitchen where everyone was standing round awkwardly – except Lottie, who was darting excitedly between them offering cheese puffs from an overflowing bowl.

'Here she is!' said Dad.

I barely recognised my dad. His stubble was gone, the baggy beach shorts and yukky sandals he'd worn all summer had been replaced by jeans with big turn-ups and shiny black Doc Marten boots, and he'd done something to his hair to make it look all sticky-uppy.

'Mel, this is Clem. Clem, this is Mel.' Dad squeezed my shoulder.

'Hi.' I forced a smile.

Mel gave me a cheery wave. 'Hi Clem, it's *so* nice to meet you.'

Mel had shoulder-length curly hair, skin that was a lighter shade of brown than Callum's, bright red lipstick and a T-shirt that said 'Love Love Love' on it, that was completely cringe.

'And you guys already know each other, don't you?' Mel

mussed up Callum's flat-top hairdo, making him flinch with embarrassment. *Hah!* Although if I were him, I'd be more embarrassed about the T-shirt he was wearing. (It had a goofy cartoon shark on it, which reminded me of a pair of pyjamas I had when I was three).

'Yeah, we're in the same class,' I said as boldly as I could.

'Yeah,' mumbled Callum, avoiding my eyes.

'And your dad was saying you're a poet, too?' said Mel. 'I'd love to see some of your poems! I bet Cal would too, wouldn't you, Cal?'

Over my dead body.

'Oh, she's very private about her poetry these days, aren't you, Clem?' said Dad, coming to the rescue. 'Lottie, on the other hand, would be only too pleased to give you a taekwondo demonstration, right, Lots?'

Phew! Saved by an only-too-happy-to-show-off little sister.

Lottie leant back, ready to give a high kick.

'WAIT!' Dad removed the bowl of cheese puffs from her hands.

'Wow! Amaaaazing!' gushed Mel as Lottie high-kicked the air and spun round. 'Wouldn't want to meet *you* down a dark alley!'

People always made a 'dark alley' comment whenever Lottie demoed her taekwondo. I went to exchange an eye-roll with her, but she cracked her knuckles in my face and gave me an icy glare. Oops – I'd forgotten about yanking her hair yesterday.

'Right, Norris clan, can you lay the table?' said Dad, turning back to the oven where a large chicken was roasting. 'Clem, put a jug of water out, would you?'

While we busied ourselves putting cutlery on the table, Callum wandered around our kitchen peering closely at everything, like he was some kind of inspector. *Moron*.

'Can't find the jug,' I mumbled.

'In my room,' said Lottie, throwing cheese puffs up in the air and catching them in her mouth.

Prickling with annoyance, I stomped upstairs, snatched the jug from Lottie's room, stomped back down and topped it up from the kitchen tap. Meanwhile, Callum had stopped by the dining table and was staring at the giant *God Save the Queen* poster on the wall.

'Like it?' asked Dad.

Callum shrugged.

'It's the artwork from an old record cover,' Dad explained.

'I *love* it,' said Mel. 'I was watching that Kirsty Allsopp

Christmas programme on TV last year and noticed she had the exact same one on her wall.'

'Did she?' Dad smiled awkwardly and opened a bottle of wine, while I plonked the jug of water on the table.

'It's almost ready,' said Dad. 'Take a pew, everyone. Callum, help yourself to water.'

I watched Callum as he sauntered over to the table, pulled out a chair and sat down. It annoyed me that he didn't seem in the slightest bit phased by being in my house. He just looked bored and annoyed rather than nervous and uncomfortable. And I *so* wanted him to feel nervous and uncomfortable. Or at the very least, impressed and slightly jealous.

'Um, excuse me?' Callum pointed to the glass jug. 'There's a goldfish in here.'

Everyone turned to look at the jug.

'MR MIYAAAAGIIIIIIIIIIII!' screamed Lottie.

'For goodness' sake!' huffed Dad, swiftly removing the jug from the table. 'Did you seriously forget to put him back in his tank?'

Lottie snatched the jug from Dad and bolted back upstairs.

'Gross,' said Callum.

'Personally, I *love* goldfish cordial!' Mel snorted with laughter.

My eyes bulged at the sound of Mel inhaling, then letting out a loud, warbly neigh like a cartoon horse, followed quickly by another one: *Snort. Inhale. Neeeeigh. Neeeeigh.* Callum shrank back in his seat.

Hoorah! *It seemed my enemy had a weak spot!*

'Sorry about that!' said Dad, placing a steaming roast chicken on the table. 'This house is like living in a zoo sometimes.'

'SQUAWK!'

'What was that?' said Mel, cocking her ear to the ceiling.

'That's my phone,' I said quickly. 'I've got a new jungle ringtone. It's plugged into my speaker upstairs.'

'Love it!' snorted Mel. 'By the way, does anyone know how to get rid of an earworm?'

Lottie and I looked at her with horror and shuffled back in our seats. I did *not* want to catch anything with the word 'worm' in it, thank you very much.

Dad laughed. 'Relax, kids. An earworm is when you get a song stuck in your head.' He turned to Mel. 'Lottie gets 'Ding Dong Merrily on High' stuck in her head regularly throughout the year, don't you, Lots? And before we know

it, we're all singing it.'

Mel neighed. 'Well, I've had that utterly dreadful 'Black Magic' song stuck in my head for days now – it's driving me insane. I think it's by Ariana Grande? No – Katy Perry maybe?'

How very DARE she!

Dad touched my arm lightly. 'Oh, I don't know, it's not so bad,' he said, squirming in his seat and blinking like he had something in his eye.

I stared daggers at her. 'You mean Little Mix?'

'Oh,' said Mel, giving Dad a worried look. 'No, no, I meant 'Black Magic Woman' – that dreadful Fleetwood Mac song from way, way back. Horrendous!' She grimaced.

Dad burst out laughing. 'Yeah, you wouldn't wanna get *that* stuck in your noggin, kids!'

'Aaggh! It's back!' shrieked Mel, snorting and neighing.

Yeah, right. I know exactly what you meant. Stop being so fake.

Dad and Mel started singing, laughing and jiggling about in their seats. Lottie giggled along with them, but I didn't think they were being the slightest bit funny. The Neighing One had just insulted my favourite pop group followed by my intelligence. Meanwhile, Callum looked like he was counting down the seconds till he could go home.

'Finish what's on your plate, Cal,' whispered Mel.

'I don't like roast chicken,' he replied. 'I only like chicken the way Dad does it.'

It was tempting to let out a loud sigh, but I managed to restrain myself.

'No worries,' smiled Dad. 'I hear your dad's a very talented chef.'

'He runs a top Jamaican restaurant,' said Callum proudly. '*And* he owns a gym now, too!'

'Wow,' said Dad. 'Cooks *and* keeps fit! Your dad sounds like a talented guy!' He winked at Mel.

'Yes, he has a lot to keep him busy,' said Mel, looking thoughtful.

'Shall I clear the table?' I interrupted, standing up and carrying mine and Lottie's plates to the dishwasher.

'Gosh, Clem. How very proactive of you,' said Dad, looking surprised. 'Don't worry – I'll clear up. Why don't you and Lottie show Callum into the living room and find a game to play?'

Callum and I avoided eye contact.

'Yay!' cheered Lottie. 'We could play 'Operation'!

Or 'Mouse Trap'!'

Mel stacked up the remaining plates on the table. 'Blimey!' she said, looking out of the window. 'There's a woman dressed like a canary over there.' She neighed as I spotted Ingrid, dressed head to toe in yellow, leaving her house with Eddie Two-Balls.

'Oh, that's our very unique neighbour, Ingrid,' said Dad. 'She's lovely, isn't she, kids?'

'Yes,' I said, through clenched teeth. 'She's super, *super* nice.'

'Ah yes, she looks nice,' Mel backtracked, carrying the stack of plates to the dishwasher and grinning at my dad.

Dad nudged me and nodded towards the living room, my cue to vamoose. *Fine*. But Callum had better make an effort to be nice, or else. I plodded after Lottie, who skipped merrily into the living room. Out of the corner of my eye, I saw Mel giving Callum an impatient nudge in our direction.

'What shall we play?' asked Lottie, kneeling next to the stack of board games piled up by the TV. 'We've got 'Mouse Trap', 'Operation', 'Ludo' – or we could watch *Moana*!'

'NOT *Moana*,' I said firmly. (Not only did I not want Callum thinking I was into Disney films, but Lottie had made us watch it so many times I never wanted to see it again).

'Don't you have an Xbox?' said Callum, as if not having an Xbox made you weirder than an alien from outer space.

'Nope,' said Lottie. 'We've got a Wii, but it doesn't work any more.'

Callum rolled his eyes and gazed around the room.

''*Harry Potter Monopoly*'?' he snorted, pointing at one of the board games. 'Aren't you a bit old for Harry Potter?'

'Aren't you a bit old to be wearing a T-shirt with a goofy shark on it?' I shot back. Seriously – who did he think he was? Even my dad loved reading Harry Potter, and he was properly OLD.

'It's a surf brand, stupid – I'm into surfing. And at least I have a style. What do you call *that*?' Callum eyed me up and down, smirking at my clothes.

'I call it *being individual*,' I said, remembering what Ingrid said once when a passer-by laughed at her pink dungarees. 'What's your problem, anyway?' I said, anger rising up inside me. 'You're a guest in my house – you should be polite.'

'Let's play 'Operation'!' said Lottie, trying to distract us from our argument. 'I'll just make sure all the pieces are in the box.'

'I didn't *ask* to be a guest in your house,' said Callum, ignoring her.

'And I didn't *ask* you to come, but we only have to put up with each other for an hour or so and then you can go home. Surely you can be nice for like *an hour*?'

Callum took a step towards me and suddenly seemed six inches taller. 'Firstly, *Tangerine*, or whatever your name is, *London's* my home – not this stupid place. I didn't ask to move down here and join that stupid school in this stupid town. And *secondly*, if my mum starts going out with your dad, it won't be just an hour or so we have to put up with each other, will it?' His eyes drifted towards my checked waistcoat. 'Or haven't you worked that out yet, Sherlock?'

I looked to Lottie for backup, but she was busy counting plastic bones – or pretending to be. So much for being a freedom fighter.

'They're just friends,' I said. 'They're not boyfriend and girlfriend – not yet, anyway.'

'And they're not going to be,' snapped Callum. 'Because *my* parents are going to get back together.'

CHAPTER 4

LATER THAT AFTERNOON

AFTER THE DREADED DUO HAD LEFT, DAD HANDED
ME A TEA TOWEL TO HELP WITH THE DRYING UP AND
FLICKED THE KETTLE ON TO MAKE A CUP OF TEA.
'SO . . . HOW DID IT GO WITH CALLUM?' HE ASKED.

'Terrible,' I said, drying up a saucepan. 'When we went
in the living room, he was grumpy, rude and couldn't wait to
leave. And, just so you know, he said his parents are going
to get back together.'

No point beating around the bush. The sooner Dad
realised his 'friendship' with Mel was doomed, the better –
for everyone involved. Particularly me.

Dad raised his eyebrows, but didn't look surprised. 'Oh dear. Sounds like Callum's having a tough time accepting their separation. Apparently, he's still hoping they'll get back together, but they already tried that once and it didn't work.'

'So, they're *not* getting back together?' My heart plummeted.

'Not according to Mel.' Dad opened the cupboard. 'Ah, no cups – *again*. I wonder where they're all hiding?' He looked at me expectantly.

'So d'you think you and Mel will become boyfriend and girlfriend?' I asked, positive that after all that snorting and neighing, the answer surely had to be a Big Fat *No Way*.

Dad chuckled. 'Give us a chance, Clem. Like I said, it's early days. I promise I'll keep you in the loop.'

I no longer felt reassured.

'But do you *like* her?' I persisted.

'Holy Arctic rolly! What is this – the Spanish Inquisition?'

I wasn't sure what the Spanish Inquisition was but I guessed he meant I was asking too many questions.

'Yes, if you must know, I like her,' he said.

But *he* wasn't getting what *I* meant. I may have been just a few weeks away from my eleventh birthday but even I knew there was a difference between *like* and *LIKE*.

'What I mean is, where is she on a scale of one to ten? Like, if one is *'Ugh – she's cringe'* and ten is *'Wow – she's supercalifragilsticexpialamazeballs'*?'

Dad threw his head back and laughed. 'Do I have to answer that?'

I folded my arms and eyeballed him.

He sighed. 'OK then, she's a nine.'

NINE?

NEIGH-NEIGH WAS A NINE?

The uneasy feeling was suddenly back – and twice as strong.

'Back in a minute,' said Dad. 'Going on a cup hunt.'

I barely heard him. This was not the number I'd hoped to hear. I'd expected a six-and-a-half tops. I could work with six and a half. Nine didn't feel like Mel was just a friend. Nine was a flashing red light. Nine sounded like love was in the air. Nine was . . . *a very worrying situation indeed.*

A situation . . . that needed to be stopped in its tracks.

Not that I didn't want my dad to have a girlfriend. Of course I knew that someday it would eventually happen – after all, Mum had been with Simon for a while now and although he had some weird habits (like popping out to buy milk in his onesie pyjamas), he was really nice.

But Dad's girlfriend could not be Mel, the woman who insulted the awesomeness that is Little Mix. The woman who called Ingrid a canary. THE WOMAN WHO NEIGHED WHEN SHE LAUGHED. And most worryingly of all, the woman who'd given birth to a creature more evil than the Green Goblin and Voldemort combined. I mean, when you're the mother of Satan, should you really be laughing at all? I think not.

Something needed to be done.

'Um, Clementine!' Dad shouted from upstairs. 'Can you come up here, please? IMMEDIATELY!'

I froze. Perrie! The game was up.

I hurried upstairs.

How long since I last checked on Perrie? Half an hour? An hour? Had she covered my room in splats of poo? Or had she decided she wanted to go home and thrown herself at my closed bedroom window, losing all her feathers in a bid for freedom? Or had Fred got into my room and eaten Perrie alive? Oh no! What was I thinking keeping a parrot hidden in my room?

I pushed open my door, bracing myself for a gut-wrenching scene of bones and feathers. However, everything looked pretty much as I'd left it and I couldn't see Perrie anywhere.

Dad folded his arms. 'Tell me, Clementine. What is in this room that clearly *shouldn't* be in this room?'

Well, obviously, an escaped scarlet macaw, *but where was she?* I looked all around me, but she was nowhere to be seen.

'Take your time,' said Dad wearily.

'I was going to—'

'*Going to?*' he interrupted me. 'You were *going to* take them back downstairs and put them in the dishwasher? *Going to*, but *didn't.*'

He pointed to a small mountain of dirty cups, glasses and plates that had formed on my desk since yesterday.

I was in trouble for *that? Woohoo* and *yabbadabbadoo*! My heart filled with joy.

'You think that's funny?' said Dad. 'I'm FED UP of nagging you about this.'

A flash of colour above me caught my eye, and I spotted Perrie perched on my bedroom light shade, a few centimetres above Dad's head.

'I'm fed up of running out of cups because they're all up here sprouting mould. From now on, you're banned from bringing anything other than a glass of water into your room. Understand?'

'*Bing bong!*'

Dad glared at me. 'Who said that?'

'It's my new message alert—'

'*Bing bong! Bing bong! Bing bong! SQUAWK!*'

Dad's jaw fell open as he tilted his head up towards my bedroom light.

At that moment, Perrie cocked her head and pooed – *right into Dad's mouth.*

'GAAAAAAARGH!' Dad went tearing from my room into the bathroom. I ran after him and watched in horror as he turned the tap on full force and held his mouth under it, making retching sounds. Then he grabbed a bottle of antiseptic mouthwash from the cabinet, took a giant slurp and gargled with all his might.

Ten minutes later, me, Dad and Lottie stood in a row watching Perrie hop along my bookcase, using my cuddly toys' heads as stepping stones.

'What in God's name is a parrot doing in your room?' said Dad, his breath reeking of antiseptic and toothpaste.

'Can he be mine?' swooned Lottie. 'I want to call him

Hei Hei, after the chicken in *Moana*.'

'*She's mine*,' I said. '*You* have Mr Miyagi.'

'How d'you know it's a she?' asked Lottie.

'How d'you know it's a he?' I retorted.

'We're not keeping it,' said Dad. 'Because it's not ours to keep. I'm phoning the RSPB to see if anyone's reported a missing parrot.'

'But we can keep her until we find the owner, can't we?' I asked.

'No, Clementine, we can't. I've got enough responsibilities without worrying about a parrot pooing all over the house or an eternally hungry geriatric cat ripping it to shreds and eating it. My work suffers from enough interruptions as it is and besides, we can't afford any more pets.' Dad headed towards my bedroom door, then paused. '*It pooed in my mouth* for pity's sake!'

'But Dad!' I protested. 'You always say that the two people you love most in the world both pooed on you!'

'Not in my mouth, Clementine. *Not in my mouth*.'

Just then, the doorbell rang and Dad plodded downstairs to answer it.

'Say *Hello Lottie*!' said Lottie, stroking Perrie's head.

'Punk is dead! *SQUAWK!*' replied Perrie.

We heard Ingrid's voice in the doorway.

'Did you take in a parcel for me today, Ray?'

'Ah yes, here you go,' replied Dad. 'Hey, come and see what we've got upstairs, Ingrid! You're gonna love this.' Two sets of footsteps came trotting up the stairs and my bedroom door swung open.

Ingrid was wearing a T-shirt with a bright yellow smiley face on it, a yellow feather boa round her neck, yellow tights and her hair in yellow fluffy space buns. 'It's my first-day-of-term outfit,' she chuckled, seeing my face. 'Just trying it on for tomorrow. You know, to put the littluns at ease.'

I wished Neigh-Neigh was here now, so she could feel bad for saying Ingrid looked like a canary.

Dad gestured dramatically towards Perrie. 'Ingrid, this is Parrot. Parrot, this is Ingrid.'

'*Bing bong!*' chirped Perrie.

'Oh, my freakin' fishnets!' squealed Ingrid. 'Aren't you a babe? I'm guessing you've borrowed her from Lyn or are there now two parrots living on our street?'

'Lyn?' we all said in unison. 'Lyn who?'

'Lyn at number one near the corner shop? You know – moved in a few months ago. She took in a parcel for me a while back and when I went to collect it, she came to the

door with a parrot on her shoulder. A parrot *just like this one*.'

My heart sank.

'Mystery solved,' said Dad. 'Thanks, Ingrid. You've been very helpful.'

'Wait – you mean Lyn doesn't know it's here?' said Ingrid.

'It flew in the window,' said Lottie. 'Clem was airing her room out cos it smelt really farty.'

I shoved my sister out the way and turned to Ingrid. 'Do you know what her name is?'

Ingrid scratched her head. 'I think she said it was Viv.'

Viv? That was a dumb name for a parrot! What kind of person was this Lyn if she named a parrot Viv and then lost it? I had a feeling I wasn't going to like her.

'And, if I remember rightly, she's a *he*,' said Ingrid.

'HAH!' Lottie gave me a triumphant look.

'Anyway, I'd better be going.' She held up her parcel and gave it a shake. 'There should be a Victorian chimney sweep costume in here, with any luck.'

We followed Dad and Ingrid out on to the landing and watched as they went downstairs.

'I bet Lyn'll be relieved to get her parrot back,' said Ingrid, pausing as Dad held the door open for her. 'I'm surprised she hasn't put missing posters all over the street.

To be honest, I found her a bit . . . what's the word? *Aloof*.
Laters!'

'Bye, Ingrid.' Dad closed the front door behind her.

I ran downstairs and grabbed him by the sleeves. 'What
does aloof mean?'

'Er, stand-offish. A bit cold, maybe?' said Dad, releasing
himself from my grip. 'But we haven't met her yet so we
shouldn't judge her. Maybe she was having a bad day?'

'I don't like her!' I wailed. 'She lost her parrot, gave it a
stupid name and she's *alooooof*!'

'Calm down, Clementine. I suggest you go and spend a
few final minutes with Viv, because it's time for us to take
him home.'

I stomped back upstairs to my room.

'Me and Perrie – I mean, Viv – need a few minutes alone,'
I said to Lottie.

Amazingly she didn't argue but sauntered out of my
room in silence.

I stroked Viv's head. 'I want you to know that if you're
not happy living with Lyn, you can come back any time.
I'll leave my window open every day, OK?'

'*Bing bong!*' came the reply.

I was curious to know what this Lyn person was like,

because so far, she sounded like a total nutcase. One thing was for sure – she'd better look after Viv properly or she'd have *me* to answer to.

CHAPTER 5

HALF AN HOUR LATER . . .

DAD AND I STOOD ON LYN'S DOORSTEP, CARRYING PERRIE — I MEAN, VIV — IN FRED'S EXTRA-LARGE CAT BASKET.

'Sounds like no one's home,' said Dad, pressing the doorbell again.

I prayed he was right. As he pressed the bell a third time, I noticed the front door looked like it wasn't closed properly. I nudged Dad and pointed.

Dad pushed the door open. 'Hello? Anyone home?'

Still no answer. This was starting to feel creepy.

'Maybe she's gone on holiday?' I said. 'And forgot to

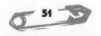

close the door properly.'

'Or maybe she's been burgled?' said Dad, pushing the door open all the way. I followed him into the hallway. 'Hello?' Dad called again. 'Anyone home? Your door was open!'

We stood at the bottom of the stairs and looked around. The walls were covered in framed record covers and what looked like awards.

'Look, Dad!' I pointed to an album cover that I recognised from Dad's old record collection. I read the title out. "Lyn Ferno: *Black Eye Suits Ya, Mate*'. You've got that one, haven't you, Dad?'

But Dad was too busy studying the next frame along which contained a shiny gold disc with some writing in the middle. I read it over his shoulder: *This 24-carat, gold-plated record is presented to Lyn Ferno in recognition of outstanding achievement and worldwide success.*

Dad swore under his breath. I giggled.

'Unless I'm very much mistaken, this is *Lyn Ferno's* house,' he gasped, his jaw hanging so low he could've swallowed a bus. I looked from the gold disc to Dad's shocked face and back. '*We're actually standing in Lyn Ferno's house!*' he repeated, a glazed look in his eyes.

'Was she a pop star when you were a boy?' I asked.

52

'She was more than just a pop star, Clem. She was a flipping PUNK LEGEND!' Dad's eyes bulged out of their sockets. 'You know how excited you were when I took you to see Little Mix last year? Lyn Ferno's my Little Mix. One of her songs came on the radio in the car the other day. You told me to turn it down, remember?'

I remembered. 'That's cos it was RUBBISH,' I said.

'*SSSSSHHHH!*' Dad hissed at me, pressing his finger to his lips.

'Why didn't Ingrid tell us it was *Lyn Ferno*?' I asked.

'She probably didn't know that Lyn is actually Lyn Ferno. Ingrid must be in her late twenties? Lyn Ferno was famous before Ingrid was even born – and she hasn't made a record in decades. If you're not familiar with her face, you probably wouldn't recognise her. And besides, you wouldn't expect a punk legend to be living on our ordinary little street. Maybe she's fallen on hard times?'

'Punk is dead!' chirped Viv.

'Dad!' I gasped. 'Maybe Viv is trying to tell us something? That's like the fifth time he's said, 'punk is dead'. What if Lyn Ferno's *dead*?'

Dad's eyes widened. 'I'd better take a look around. You stay here.'

'HELLO!' he shouted. 'IS ANYONE HOME? We've got your parrot!'

From where we were standing, we could see the kitchen was empty. Through the half-open door to the front room, I could see some large brown boxes with labels on saying 'front room'. Dad poked his head round the living-room door, nodded towards the staircase and hollered. 'I'm bringing your parrot upstairs!' He went upstairs with the cat basket and paused at the top. I tiptoed up behind him. At the end of the landing, a door was ajar.

'You were supposed to wait downstairs,' whispered Dad. 'Wait here.' He made his way along the landing with Viv and knocked loudly on the bedroom door. 'Lyn? Are you in there? Are you OK? I'm your neighbour from down the road. I've got your parrot. May I come in?'

Dad pushed open the door to reveal a large creamy-coloured bedroom with a king-sized bed in the middle, a tall, twisty, wooden parrot perch and a throne-like armchair covered in Union Jack material. I tiptoed up behind him again – curiosity had got the better of me.

Poking out from beneath a shiny black duvet was a bed-heady halo of spiky orange hair.

I inhaled and squeezed Dad's arm, making him jump.

54

'*How?* You heard him – his mum'll be super-annoyed, she'll probably tell my dad and then I'll probably be grounded or something.'

Rom smiled. 'Yeah, but if his mum thinks you're a *trouble-maker*, won't that make things a bit awkward between her and your dad?'

I took in what Rom had just said. *She was right!* Neigh-Neigh would believe I was a monster (totally ridonculous) while Dad would believe Callum was exaggerating the incident just to make me look bad (totally the truth). AWKWARD!

I gave my best friend a big hug. 'Romola Granola, you're a total genius!'

'I know!' she laughed.

'O. M. *ACTUAL* G! She's *dead*!' I felt a bit queasy.

Dad put the cat basket down and nervously approached the side of the bed. He took a deep breath, reached a trembling hand towards the body and gave it a gentle nudge.

Nothing.

He nudged her a bit harder and suddenly there was a long, loud snort, making us jump out of our skins.

'Whoa!' Dad tripped over something and stumbled backwards, knocking into the parrot perch. I caught the perch before it fell and moved the pair of multi-coloured roller skates that Dad had tripped over.

When we next looked at the body in the bed, a pair of bloodshot eyes were blinking at us from just above the duvet.

'You're alive!' I said, relieved.

'*Of course* I'm alive.' She pushed the duvet down to reveal a pale wrinkly face with shadowy eye bags. 'Who the hell are you?'

Dad was just standing there staring at her like she was a monkey in a zoo. He seemed to have fallen into some kind of trance, so I took over.

'We've brought your parrot back – look!' I picked up the cat basket, opened the hatch and helped Viv out.

Viv squawked, spread his wings and flew straight to his perch.

'*Back?* What do you mean *back?* And you still haven't answered my question – who the hell are you and where's Pascal?'

'I'm Clementine and this is my dad, Ray. He's a MEGA fan of yours.'

Lyn rolled her eyes.

'That *is* your parrot, isn't it?' I pointed to Viv.

She looked at me like I was mad. 'Of course it is!'

'It's just that I found him in my bedroom yesterday.' I recounted the whole story (minus the reason why my window was open).

Lyn hauled herself up into a sitting position, revealing a paw-print nightdress. She folded her arms. 'I take it you didn't meet a young skinny French man downstairs by the name of Pascal?'

'No,' I said. (Dad was still in a trance.)

'Absolutely useless,' Lyn pursed her lips. 'You simply can't get the staff these days.' She looked at me. 'Pascal's my assistant. I wasn't aware Vivian was missing – and now I've got two intruders in my bedroom, I fear Pascal's days may be numbered.' She peered over the side of her bed. 'Where the hell are my roller skates?'

Dad snapped out of his trance and reached for the roller skates, placing them on the floor next to the bed. Lyn swung her legs out from under the duvet, slipped her feet into the roller skates, picked up a long thick rope that was coming from an en suite bathroom and dragged herself along the floorboards towards it. Dad and I watched in amazement as she rolled into her bathroom and closed the door.

The next thing we heard was a loud fart. I clapped my hands over my mouth to muffle my laughter. Even Dad was struggling to keep a straight face.

'We should probably go,' whispered Dad, coming to his senses and turning towards the bedroom door.

'We should at least say goodbye first,' I said, holding him back.

The bathroom door opened and Lyn rolled out, still clutching the rope.

'Thanks for bringing Vivian back,' she smiled. 'I appreciate it. Sorry if I seemed rude – you just gave me a bit of a fright, that's all.'

'You gave us quite a fright too,' said Dad, finding his voice again. 'We thought you were dead.'

'Not yet,' grumbled Lyn. 'Clementine, is it?'

I nodded.

'Well, if you'd like to come and visit Vivian some time, Clementine, you'd be more than welcome. I'm afraid I'm not the greatest company these days and Vivian does love to talk. If Pascal's not here, then there's a spare key under the cactus out front. Just let yourself in – if that's OK with Dad?' She glanced at Dad.

'Er, yeah, sure,' he replied. 'Um, before we go, may I ask—'

'I don't do autographs any more.'

'No, I was going to ask why the roller skates?'

'Oh. I don't want my feet to touch the ground. I'm having a bed-in, you see. Continuity is paramount.'

'What's a bed-in?' I frowned.

Lyn pointed to a book on her bedside table. 'I read this novel about a woman who goes to bed for a year and I thought, what a brilliant idea! *I'm* going to do that. The last few years have been a bit . . . overwhelming. So, I'm having a holiday – in my bed.'

'But why can't you let your feet touch the ground?' I asked.

'Well I *could* let them touch the ground if I wanted, but that would be the slippery slope that leads me downstairs and back to normal life – and I don't want normal life at the moment. I want my bed. Pascal feeds and waters me, opens

my post and stuff, so the only thing I need to get out of bed for is the old *pee-pee, plop-plop*.'

I tried not to giggle. 'Are showers allowed?'

'PAH! Hygiene's overrated.' Lyn sat on her bed and slid her roller skates off. 'Anyone fancy a humbug?' She picked up a packet of sweets from her bedside table and offered them to us. We both shook our heads, although I would've taken one if Dad had.

'What about when your friends come over? Do you just watch Netflix in bed?' I had so many questions all of a sudden!

'I don't have many friends these days,' said Lyn. 'And I prefer it that way. But like I said, you'd be welcome to come and visit Viv, Clementine.'

'Thank you,' I beamed.

'We should probably leave you in peace. It was nice to meet you, Lyn,' said Dad. 'Sorry we gave you a fright.'

'Ah, I'm a tough old bird, me.' Lyn eased herself back under her duvet. 'If you see Pascal on your way out, tell him I'd like a word, would you?'

I nodded. 'Bye, then. Bye Viv!'

It wasn't until we were back in our house that Dad finally spoke.

'Did I imagine all that, Clem? Or did that *actually* happen?'

I squeezed Dad's hand. He was in a state of shock. To be honest, I sort of was, too. It's not every day you meet an ex-famous person who owns a parrot and wears roller skates to go to the loo.

'I can't wait to tell Mel,' he said.

Damn. I hadn't thought about the Dreaded Duo *once* since we'd entered Lyn's house.

'What a character!' said Dad. 'What did you make of her, Clem?'

Lyn Ferno was without doubt the oddest person I'd ever met. So odd, she even made Ingrid seem ordinary.

'What is a punk, anyway?' I asked.

'Well,' said Dad, 'Punk music started in the 1970s, when I was a kid. It was fast, loud and angry, with lyrics that criticised society, the government or the Queen.'

'Did Lyn Ferno criticise the Queen?'

'No. Her lyrics mainly had a feminist theme – she wanted to show that men and women are equal.'

Of course they're equal – *duh*!

'Anyway, music aside,' Dad continued, 'her other main claim to fame was for burping on a prime time TV show.'

'Was it a big burp or a little accidental burp?'

'It was an epic burp. It lasted eight seconds, spanned an entire octave and was most definitely deliberate. Terry Wogan's face was priceless.' Dad grinned. 'Nan and Granddad thought she was awful, but I worshipped her.'

I wasn't sure *what* to make of her. There was something about her that puzzled me – mainly, what made a person want to go to bed for a *whole year*? And, if she was famous, why wasn't she living in a mansion with a swimming pool? Why didn't she want friends visiting her? And, most importantly, could she be trusted to look after Viv properly? Clearly, I would have to visit Viv to find out.

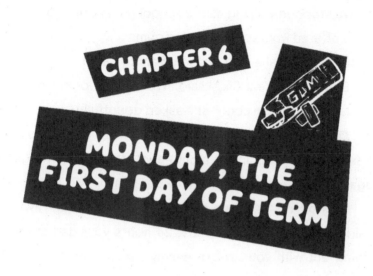

CHAPTER 6

MONDAY, THE FIRST DAY OF TERM

ROM HAD RETURNED FROM ITALY WITH A YELLOW
AND PURPLE BRAID THREADED INTO HER LONG
DARK HAIR, NEW GOLD STUDS IN HER EARLOBES
AND HER SKIN LOOKED LIKE IT'D CAUGHT THE SUN.
AS SOON AS SHE'D TIED A SOUVENIR FRIENDSHIP
BRACELET ON MY WRIST, WE SET OFF FROM THE
CORNER SHOP, (WHICH, AT ROUGHLY A HUNDRED
METRES FROM BOTH OUR FRONT DOORS, WAS THE
PERFECT MEETING PLACE NOW THAT WE COULD
WALK TO SCHOOL BY OURSELVES), WITH ME
UPDATING HER ON ALL MY LATEST NEWS.

We stopped walking as the school gates came into view and I offered Rom some chewing gum.

'Better not,' she said. 'I don't want to get in trouble.'

'But we're in Year Six,' I said. 'We need to look *cool*.'

'Is chewing gum cool?' she asked doubtfully.

'*Duh – yes!*' I couldn't explain how – it just was. I popped a few Arctic Mints in my mouth and offered her the gum again, but my sensible BFF shook her head.

'So nothing happened the whole time I was away,' said Rom, 'and then in the last 24 hours your dad started going out with your sworn enemy's mum, you rescued a parrot that pooed in your dad's mouth and met a famous rock star who wears roller skates to the loo?' She looked a bit baffled.

Of course, put like that, it sounded like I'd made it all up.

'You *do* believe me, don't you?' I panicked.

'Yes, of course I do!' said Rom. 'So, are you going to visit Perrie – I mean, Viv?'

We carried on walking slowly towards school.

'Definitely. Lyn's a bit . . . *on Planet Mermicorn*, as Lots calls it. She said she's got an assistant called Pascal, but he's obviously not doing a very good job of looking after either of them if Viv can get out and we can get in.'

'Maybe you could offer to look after Viv for a while?' Rom said hopefully. 'We could teach him to say cool things.'

I sighed. 'Dad would never agree.'

'But if he's all slushy-mushy with his new girlfriend, he might change his mind.' She waggled her eyebrows.

'I don't want him to get all slushy-mushy with her,' I said, alarmed. 'I mean, why *her*? Callum Harvey's mum of *all* people? Why couldn't he choose someone else?'

'Good point,' said Rom. 'I wouldn't want Callum as my step-brother either.'

The word 'step-brother' sent shivers down my spine. 'Dad's sort-of-girlfriend's son' was scary enough, but step-brother? *No. NOOO!*

'Clem? You OK?' Rom touched my arm. I'd stopped walking and chewing and was staring into space without realising it. 'Wait, *step-brother*'s the wrong word. Like you said, they're just friends at the moment, right? My Uncle Samir has a new girlfriend every few months. He's always telling us he's met The One but three months later, he's met someone else!'

I know Rom was trying to comfort me, but the way Dad had been acting lately, I had a bad feeling about him and Neigh-Neigh. A feeling that things were about to turn a lot slushier and a lot mushier.

'They *have* to break up,' I said. 'Or my life's going to be hell.'

'Stop worrying, Clem!' Rom took my arm and dragged me towards school. 'Everything'll turn out fine. Come on – we've got Mr C, so it's not all bad.'

Mr C (officially Mr Campbell, but no one called him that – not even the other teachers) had grown a short beard over the summer holidays and was wearing a trilby hat, baggy combats and neon orange trainers. A chunky silver chain dangled from his belt and back up into his pocket. We had totally lucked out being in his class. That was because there were three classes in each year in Ferndale Primary, so you never knew which teacher you'd end up with – and everyone wanted to have Mr C in Year Six.

I looked up at the large flag hanging on the wall above the whiteboard. It had three wide vertical stripes: a white stripe in the middle, and a green one on either side. I'd learned from listening to previous Year Sixes that it was the flag of Nigeria, where Mr C's grandparents came from before they moved to England many years ago. I couldn't

believe I was finally sitting in his classroom.

Me and Rom grinned at each other as Ferndale Primary's most popular teacher collected all our phones in a safety box before going through the register.

As he got closer to my name, I discreetly spat my gum into my hand and stuck it underneath my desk.

'Romola Narayan?'

'Yes, sir.' Rom gave a giggly wave.

'Clementine Norris?'

'Yes, sir!' I raised my hand, sat up straight, smiled my biggest smile and let my super-amazing aura ooze out of me and surround him like the aroma of a margherita pizza, fresh out of the oven. Mr C didn't know it yet, but I was going to be one of his favourite pupils ever. He nodded and carried on.

When he was done with the register, Mr C tossed his marker pen up in the air and caught it one-handed. 'Right, everybody come and stand over here! We're going to have a little reshuffle.'

We all groaned while making our way to the front of the class, but Mr C ignored the protests and directed us to our new seats. Minutes later we'd been rearranged so that Rom and I were now sitting across a narrow aisle from Luke McDougall, whose hair had been cut so short it looked more like stubble, and Callum Harvey – who was sitting in the seat I'd just left.

Great.

If there was one person I wanted to be as far away from as possible it was Callum Doofus Harvey. He smoothed his hand over his too-cool-for-school hair and scowled at me.

'The feeling's mutual,' I mumbled.

He was about to snark back when something under his desk distracted him.

'Gross!' he cried, standing up and pointing to my impressively large wad of gum which was now welded on to his school trousers. (In hindsight, three pellets of Arctic Mint was more than my jaws could handle).

'Whose gum is that?' Mr C folded his arms. I speedily reeled my eau-de-pizza aura back into its box and went into invisibility mode.

Mr C eyeballed me over the top of his glasses. It was not the look of amazement and wonder I'd been hoping for. 'Clementine, I believe?'

'Yes?' I said innocently.

He sighed and a few people sniggered.

'And so it begins . . .' He shook his head sadly and checked the clock on the wall. '9.15 a.m. I honestly didn't expect the fun and games to kick off quite so soon. That's a new record! Right, can everyone make their way to assembly? I'll catch up with you in a minute. Clementine, come here please.'

Rom gave me a weary look as she walked past.

'So . . .' Mr C leant back in his chair and eyed me as I stood awkwardly beside his desk. 'Is there anything you'd like to say to me?'

He couldn't possibly know for sure that I was guilty, so I thought I'd win him over with my lovable, goofy charm.

'Yes, I like your trainers.'

'Good for you. And what would you like to say to me about *that*?' Mr C pointed towards the desk where I'd stuck my gum.

'Um . . .' I shifted my weight from one foot to the other.

He took off his glasses. 'Clementine, it doesn't take a rocket scientist to work out it was you. You were sitting at that desk before I asked everyone to change places. No one else has sat at that desk – or any desk – since before the summer holidays. The chewing gum you stuck there was freshly masticated. Old gum would've been dry and therefore would not have got stuck to Callum's trousers.' He polished his glasses before replacing them on his nose. 'So, I'll ask you once again: is there anything you'd like to say to me?'

I swallowed. 'What does 'masticated' mean?'

'It means chewed.'

I admired his knowledge of long words, slick detective skills and super-cool trainers in equal measure.

'You've already earnt yourself a lunchtime detention – the longer you keep me waiting, the higher your chances of an after-school detention as well.'

'I'm sorry, sir. I'm sorry I brought chewing gum into school, stuck it on a desk and got it on Callum's trousers. I didn't mean for that bit to happen.'

'Well, if his parents or carers can't get the gum *off* his trousers, you'd better warn your parents or carers they could be buying him a new pair. So, I suggest you fess up as soon as you get home.' Mr C nodded towards the door. 'Go on, get to assembly – and take note: this is a very shabby start to Year Six, Clementine. Very shabby indeed.'

I scurried off to assembly, my cheeks burning with embarrassment. So much for becoming one of Mr C's favourite pupils ever. I'd managed to achieve the opposite – in under thirty minutes! How on earth was I going to come back from this?

At break time, Rom and I were about to head off for a private talk in the far corner of the playground when Callum prodded me hard in the back. He pointed to a wet patch on his trousers where he must've tried to scrub the gum off. You could still see sticky white marks. Oops.

'You did that deliberately,' he snarled.

'No, I didn't! It was an accident. How was I to know we were all going to change places?'

'You put it there as I was walking towards the desk.'

'Yeah!' said Luke McDougall, standing behind him.

'Oh, shut up, McDonut,' said Rom. 'You're such a stirrer.'

'I didn't! I put it there just before he called my name on the register,' I said.

'My mum'll be *seriously annoyed*,' he said in a menacing voice.

'Good!' I turned my back on him, grabbed Rom and dragged her as far away from him as possible.

'Trust him to pick the biggest idiot in the class to make friends with,' sighed Rom. 'What a pair of doofuses. Or should that be *doofi*? Cactus, cacti, doofus, doofi . . . ?'

'Rom!' I wailed as soon as we were out of earshot. 'My life's going from bad to worse!'

'But Clem, this could actually work out in your favour.'

CHAPTER 7

LATER THAT DAY...

ON OUR WAY BACK FROM SCHOOL, I PERSUADED ROM TO COME TO MY HOUSE SO THAT DAD WOULDN'T BE ABLE TO GO TOO MAD AT ME WHEN THE GUM INCIDENT CAME UP.

'Just fess up,' advised Rom. 'Be honest and tell him what you did.' *Agreed. I would tell the truth.*

'I'll say it was a stupid thing to do,' I said. *Also the truth.* 'And then I'll say how desperately sorry I am about it.' *A big, fat lie.*

'Clem-Cakes! Romola Granola!' Dad greeted us cheerily as we walked through the front door. 'The kettle's on and

I've bought everyone their favourite biscuits to celebrate surviving the first day of term.'

Hmm. We wouldn't be celebrating once he heard about The Gum Incident, so I decided we'd better eat as many biscuits as we could before I confessed. We followed him into the kitchen where Lottie was sitting at the table, dunking a chocolate digestive into a cup of hot milk and sucking noisily at its soggy edge.

'Hold out your hands!' Dad threw a packet of custard creams at me. I caught them and put them on the table. He looked miffed at my lack of excitement. 'I thought those were your favourites?'

'Thanks, but I've gone off custard creams.'

'I'll have some!' Rom held out her hands and I passed her the packet.

Dad frowned. 'Oh! Right.' The penny dropped. 'You should've said. Sorry, Clemmington.'

'Why don't you like custard creams any more?' Lottie looked up, a ring of chocolate around her mouth.

Before I could give my dopey sister a snarky reminder, Rom stepped in. 'The poem Clem entered for the Ferndale Juniors poetry competition last term, which unfortunately didn't win, was about custard creams.'

'Oh.' Lottie turned back to her milk and reached for another biscuit. 'You should've written it about chocolate digestives – then you'd have won.'

I rolled my eyes. Dad passed us each a cup of milky tea.

'So, girls, how was the amazing Mr C? Did he live up to expectations?'

'He's awesome,' grinned Rom. 'He makes school really fun.'

'I'm glad to hear it,' said Dad. 'Clem? What's up? You look a bit down in the dumps.'

I stared at my feet. 'There's something I need to tell you. Please don't be angry with me.'

Dad pulled out a chair at the kitchen table and gestured for us to sit down. Time to dust off my acting skills. I thought about the lady I'd seen at the vets who was crying because she'd just been told her dog had to be put down. I imagined being told the same about Fred. My eyes and nose began to tingle and I started to mist up. Result!

'What happened?' Dad took my hand.

'I'm really sorry, Dad. I *promise* it was an accident.'

'It's true, Mr Norris,' Rom backed me up. 'Clem didn't mean for it to happen.'

I told Dad what had happened and how he might get

an angry phone call from Mel later. 'Callum said I did it *deliberately*, but I swear it wasn't like that. I was *so* looking forward to Year Six and now Mr C thinks I'm an idiot – which is fair enough – but Callum hates me more than he did already, which is *really* unfair because, until today, I hadn't even done anything wrong!'

To my surprise, real tears came trickling out of my eyes! Not bad, Clementine – acting skills fully present and in tip-top form! Rom gave me a sideways glance. I thought she might laugh, so I nudged her with my foot and willed her to keep up the act.

Dad reached out and squeezed my hand. 'Sounds like you've punished yourself enough for one day, Clem. Taking chewing gum into school was a pretty stupid thing to do, but we all make mistakes. I'll sort it with Mel. Just do me a favour – no more gum, OK?'

I nodded. 'I promise.'

'And I'll make sure she keeps that promise,' said Rom.

'Thanks, Rom. I know I can count on you.'

Oh per-leease. Sometimes Rom could suck up just a bit too much.

'But, Dad, why does Callum hate me so much?' I wiped my nose on my sleeve and looked at him with teary eyes.

'He doesn't *hate* you.' Dad reached behind him for the box of tissues next to the toaster. He put it on the table and I helped myself, dabbing at my eyes. 'He's just angry at life at the moment. I'll talk to Mel about it. See if she can have a word with him. He'll settle down eventually, I promise.' Dad got up and kissed me on the forehead. 'Why don't you go and visit Viv? Take your mind off it.'

'OK,' I agreed. 'Rom, wanna come?'

'And meet Viv?' said Rom. 'Yes please!'

'Knock first though,' said Dad. 'Don't want to risk giving her a heart attack again. And don't overstay your welcome – she won't be expecting two of you.' He threw a packet of mint humbugs at me. 'Here, thought you could give her these.'

Rom and I fist-bumped under the table. The Gum Incident was over. No matter what Callum said to Neigh-Neigh, or what Neigh-Neigh said to Dad, I was in the clear. KerPOW! *One-nil to Clementine Florentine.* Put that in your pie-hole and chomp on it, Callum Harvey.

I found the key under the cactus and was about to let myself in when I remembered to ring the doorbell first. I heard footsteps approaching.

The front door opened and a thin man in tight jeans with tattoos on his arms and lots of piercings on his ears looked down at us. 'Yes?' he said impatiently.

I guessed this must be Lyn's assistant, Pascal. He didn't seem very friendly.

'Um, I'm Clementine and this is Rom. Lyn said I could come and visit Viv. But if it's not a good time, we can come back another day?' I stepped back, thinking it might be better to come back when he wasn't there.

'Of course! *Bonjour!* Do come in!' He broke into a wide smile and ushered us inside. 'You found the naughty Vivian, *non?*'

'Yes.' I followed him into the hallway, clutching the packet of humbugs and pulling Rom along behind me.

'Clementine!' I liked the way he said my name with a French accent. 'I am very grateful to you, you know? I was *so* worried – I looked for Vivian *everywhere*. I was praying he would come back because otherwise, *mon Dieu*, Lyn would kill me!'

'How did he escape?' asked Rom, keeping her voice low in case Lyn could hear us upstairs.

'It was my mistake. *Stupid, stupid Pascal!*' He slapped his wrist and lowered his voice to a whisper. 'Her bedroom, it smelled so bad. I insisted on opening the window for a while, and I'm SURE I didn't open it enough for Viv to get out, but then, I went to make double sure and when I came back, Lyn was sleeping and Viv – gone! *Mon coeur! Mon coeur!*' He clutched his heart dramatically. 'When Lyn woke up, I told her Viv was downstairs for a change of scenery. Then I posted a photo of Viv on Facebook saying *HELP!*'

Rom and I giggled. Pascal was a lot friendlier than he'd first seemed.

'So, did she get mad at you?' I asked.

He exhaled. '*Non.* She forgave me. After she met you, Clementine, she was in a very good mood. It was unusual, because normally she is in a very *bad* mood.' He stepped aside and gestured for us to go upstairs. 'I'm sure she will be happy to see you. Go on, please.'

We went upstairs and knocked on Lyn's bedroom door, which was ajar.

'Who is it?' she said brusquely.

'Clementine,' I said. 'And my friend, Rom.'

'Come in! Don't be shy.'

I pushed the door open and we went inside.

'Hi, I'm Romola,' said Rom.

'Rom lives round the corner from the shop. She's my best friend,' I explained.

'Nice to meet you, Romola,' said Lyn. 'I like your hair braid.'

'Thank you,' said Rom, touching her hair.

Viv squawked and flapped his wings. *'Bing bong! Bing bong! Twoooooooo-weeeeeee!'*

'Someone's pleased to see you!' smiled Lyn, folding the page in her novel and placing it on the bedside table.

'Oh, he is CUTE!' Rom squealed.

'I hope it's OK me bringing Rom – I wanted her to meet Viv,' I said. 'And you, of course.'

'That's absolutely fine.' Lyn shuffled upright against her pillows and pulled her paw-print nightdress into place. Her orange spikes were bent this way and that from lying down.

'Um, these are for you,' I said, holding out the packet of humbugs.

'Oh, how very kind, thank you!' She took them from me, opened a drawer in her bedside table and dropped them in next to several other packets of humbugs. Clearly she wasn't about to run out anytime soon.

Lyn cleared her throat. 'If you pat your shoulder and say, 'stand and deliver', Viv might come and perch on you.'

'Stand and what?' I said.

'Deliver.'

'What does that mean?' asked Rom.

'It's the name of a song,' explained Lyn. 'And it's what highwaymen used to say in the olden days when they robbed rich people in their horse-drawn carriages.'

'In the olden days when you were little?' asked Rom.

'Slightly before that,' chuckled Lyn. 'A couple of centuries ago.'

'Oh,' we chorused.

I did as she said and patted my shoulder. 'Stand and deliver?'

'Louder. Hold out your arm,' said Lyn.

'STAND AND DELIVER!'

Viv flew off his perch and landed on my outstretched arm. I tickled his head while he ruffled his feathers and cooed happily.

'He likes you,' said Lyn. 'He doesn't do that for just anyone, you know.'

I felt myself glow. It felt good to know Viv liked me. I passed him to Rom and he hopped on to her arm just as her phone beeped in her pocket. 'Oh no,' she moaned. 'I forgot my cousin's coming for tea – I'd better go.' She

stroked Viv and passed him back to me before picking up her schoolbag. 'Nice to meet you, Miss Ferno,' she said.

'Please, call me Lyn,' said Lyn. 'Nice to meet you, too, Romola.'

'See you on the corner in the morning!' Rom patted me on the back as she hurried off.

'Does your dad know you're here?' Lyn asked.

'Yes,' I replied. 'The humbugs were from him really.'

'What does he do?' she asked, scratching a strip of shaved hair on the side of her scalp. 'For work, I mean.'

'He works from home. He writes stuff like newsletters and emails.'

'Sounds utterly boring.'

'Yeah, he prefers writing his music blog. He's a big fan of yours.'

'So you said. What about your mum? What does she do?'

'She runs a company that . . .' I tried to remember how Mum explained her work. 'That does marketing for hotels and stuff. She's in Hong Kong at the moment. That's why we live with our dad, cos he works from home while Mum travels a lot.'

'Your parents are divorced?'

'Yeah, but they're still friends.'

'Lucky for you. I wish my parents had got divorced. All they ever did was fight. They would've been so much happier apart.'

I wasn't sure what to say to that, so I carried on tickling Viv's head.

'They're dead now,' said Lyn, picking a bit of fluff off her nightie. 'From natural causes – gawd bless their slumbering souls.' She looked at me. 'Siblings?'

'I have a sister, Lottie. She's eight.'

'Get on with her?'

'Kind of. She's very loud and always has to have her way.'

'I used to have a sister . . .' Lyn's eyes dropped to her lap.

I waited for her to explain but instead she said: 'Pascal says I should let him get people in to decorate my room, but I can't be bothered. In the past I've always done things by myself, but I have zero motivation at the moment. He's already done the hallway – insisted on putting those silly gold discs on the wall. Anyway, what do you think?' She glanced around her bedroom.

I looked around me. The walls were a pale custardy colour, with white window frames and cream curtains. I didn't have a clue about decorating houses or what colours went well together. My mum was good at that sort of thing – she got most of her ideas from the hotels she stayed in.

'It looks OK to me,' I said.

Lyn shook her head. 'Magnolia, Clementine, is the colour of no imagination. And while I'm too old and cynical to give a flying toenail about stylish interiors, if I let Pascal have his way in here, the walls will be covered in flamingos and palm trees – which would give me a migraine. So, I was thinking . . .' Lyn opened her lower bedside drawer and rummaged among a sea of felt-tips and notepads until she pulled out a thick black marker pen, '. . . that we could have some fun. I want you to take this pen and, on this wall to your right, write in giant letters the first word that comes into your head.' She held the pen out towards me.

Write on her clean, creamy wall? *Was she serious?* I remembered Mum telling me off for drawing on the wall when I was little.

Coaxing Viv up on to my shoulder, I approached the side of her bed and took the pen from her. 'Really?' I said. 'Are you *sure* you want me to mark your wall?'

Lyn's bloodshot eyes sparkled. 'I have a long history of "improving" walls,' she said, making air quotes. 'Trust me.'

This was going to be FUN!

'Any word at all?' I asked, some very naughty words flashing before my eyes.

'*Any word at all*,' she said, raising an eyebrow.

'*Bing bong!*' sang Viv. I stared at the wall and resisted the urge to write *Bing bong*.

'Don't overthink it,' she tutted. 'I want the first word that pops into your head.'

I unscrewed the lid and placed the nib against the wall.

'*Except magnolia!*' she blurted. 'Any word in the entire English language except *magnolia*. I can't disassociate the word from the colour. Continue.'

I pressed the nib against the wall and moved it slowly up and down until I'd written a giant capital N. Then, picking up the pace, I added EIGH. I put the lid back on the pen.

'*NEIGH?*' read Lyn. She hooted with laughter. '*That* was the first word that came into your head?'

I felt a bit ridiculous. What had she been expecting me to write? She'd said, 'the first word that comes into your head' and NEIGH was it (after I'd dismissed the rude words which I didn't have the courage to write).

'Again!' said Lyn. 'Write something else!'

I tried to think.

'NO! Don't think! Just write!'

I unscrewed the lid again and wrote, Lyn's eyes following the marker as it squeaked against the smoothness of the wall.

'POEM?' she said. 'You've surprised me, Clementine. There are two words I was not expecting to see on my bedroom wall – two words I'm very fond of, as it happens. Tell me, why *neigh*?'

I wasn't sure how much I ought to tell her about Neigh-Neigh, so I simply explained that I knew someone who had a laugh like a horse.

'I see,' she chuckled. 'And why *poem*?'

'Because I like writing poems,' I shrugged.

'You do?' Lyn's face lit up. 'Then next time you come, perhaps you'd like to write one on the wall?'

I glanced at the wall. Why would she want one of my not-very-good poems written wonkily across her bedroom wall? Personally, I'd choose Pascal's flamingos and palm trees any day.

'You don't have to,' said Lyn. 'It's just that, well, look at the fabulous difference you've made to my room already with just two words!'

I sized up the large area of clear, untouched magnolia and imagined filling it from top to bottom with my words. The thought filled me with excitement. But then another thought

equally filled me with dread: that of Lyn Ferno, with her gold disc awards for worldwide success, reading one of my silly, childish poems and grabbing a tin of dreaded magnolia to put the wall back to how it was as quickly as possible.

'My poems aren't very good,' I said.

'Says who?' demanded Lyn.

'Says the judges of the Ferndale Juniors poetry competition. And the winner. And *me*.'

'I see,' said Lyn, screwing up her face as if trying to figure out a mathematical equation. She took a deep breath. 'Once upon a time, a girl called Linda Jones wrote a short story called *The Teacher from Outer Space*. She was proud of her story and couldn't wait for her English teacher to read it. But her teacher said it was average and poorly written – littered with spelling mistakes, clichés and an embarrassingly obvious ending. Linda Jones was crushed. She went home from school that day, screwed the story up into a ball, chucked it in her wastepaper basket and wept into her pillow.'

A phone beeped on the bedside table. Lyn glanced at it. 'That's Pascal telling me my tea's on its way, so we'd better say bye-bye.'

'What happened to Linda Jones's short story?'

Lyn tapped into her phone without looking up. 'If you see Pascal on your way out, please tell him I don't eat *raclette* – it's too rich. Baked beans on toast will suffice.'

I gave Viv one last tickle, placed him back on his perch and said goodbye, stepping carefully over Lyn's roller skates. I was about to close her bedroom door behind me when she called out.

'By the way, ask your dad what his favourite Lyn Ferno song is. I'd be interested to know.'

'Er, OK.' I pulled the door shut behind me feeling slightly confused.

What on earth was the point of telling me about Linda Jones? I wanted to know what happened to her and her short story. Was Lyn Ferno losing her memory? Or was she keeping me in suspense on purpose?

CHAPTER 8

THE NEXT DAY

THE SECOND I ENTERED THE CLASSROOM THE
NEXT MORNING I WAS READY TO DO BATTLE WITH
CALLUM. BUT HE HAD HIS NOSE DEEP IN A BOOK
CALLED *DEADLY SEA CREATURES* AND DIDN'T
EVEN LOOK UP AS I SWEPT PAST HIM, RESISTING
THE URGE TO SCORCH A HOLE IN HIM WITH MY
IMAGINARY MAGIC POWERS. RELIEVED THAT I
DIDN'T HAVE TO GET INTO A SNARKATHON WITH
MY ARCH-ENEMY, I RELAXED INTO MY SEAT,
JOINED SWIFTLY BY ROM WHO WAS SHAKING
ALL OVER.

'What happened?' I asked. I'd only left her in the cloak-room two minutes ago.

'Mrs Simpkins just told me off for running in the corridor!' she squeaked. 'But I wasn't! I *never* run in the corridors.'

'Ouch,' I sympathised. Being told off by Mrs Simpkins, The World's Scariest Dinner Lady who screeched like a vulture, was every Ferndale pupil's worst nightmare. But for Rom, definitely one of Ferndale's most well-behaved students, this had to be doubly painful.

I put my arm round her. 'Rom, we always knew we'd be Simpkinned one day.'

'She threatened to send me to see Mrs Barraclough! I've never been sent to Mrs Barraclough ever!' She held up a trembling hand. 'Look at me – I'm shaking.'

I stroked my friend's shoulder to calm her down. Seeing Mrs Barraclough wouldn't be nearly as scary as being told off by Mrs Simpkins, because Mrs Barraclough was not a very scary headmistress. But with Romola, it was the idea of a stain on her immaculate school record that hurt the most.

'You OK, Romola?' asked Mr C as he strode into the classroom wearing a pair of super-cool, bright-green Nikes.

Rom nodded.

'OK. Good morning 6C!'

As Mr C went through the register, I wondered how many different pairs of brightly coloured trainers he owned. I wanted to ask him but knew I wouldn't have the courage to say a single word to him until I was back in his good books again – which I was hoping would be soon, as from now on I was in maximum angelic mode and on a mission to make my halo of goodness glow so brightly it'd be visible from outer space.

I'd been smiley and polite to all my fellow classmates, quiet and well-behaved around all members of staff and, as well as trying hard to *look* studious, I'd also tried hard to actually *be* studious, concentrating on my work and putting effort into every single subject – *even maths*.

After completing the register, Mr C made an announcement about some updates to the school website and a reminder to keep our lunch money cards topped up. Then he walked round to the front of his desk, tilted his trilby hat up and, looking down his nose, gave us all a cold, hard stare – as if he was planning on making us do a hundred laps of the playground to wake our brains up.

Then he started tapping his foot and clicking his fingers. His hips started to sway and his head started to nod like a pigeon. Rom and I tried not to giggle – not because we

thought Mr C looked silly, but because we never knew what
he was going to do next. He opened his mouth.

'Listen up kids, I got something to tell ya
You all need a bath cos I'm starting to smell ya
Nah, I'm just kiddin' it's nothin' that serious
It's just when I start rapping I start getting delirious

So anyway, we're gonna have a little competition
You don't have to enter – it's of your own volition
You may already know that I'm a sucker and a nerd
When it comes to having fun with the *Spoken Word*

Haikus, songs and poems, plays and short stories,
Take some words you love and give them some glory
Get inspired by a movie or a book on a shelf
Then have a go at writing something yourself

All you need to do is perform with passion
And follow your heart, not the latest fashion
Give it some fire – make the audience go
WHOAAA!
Together we can make an unforgettable show

Mr C leant back against his desk and stroked his chin. 'Any questions?'

'What's a haykey?' asked Tabitha Clarke.

'I'm so glad you asked, Tabitha,' said Mr C. 'A haiku, pronounced *hi-koo*, is a type of short poem that comes from Japan. It has seventeen syllables spread across three lines – typically five syllables in line one, seven in line two and five in line three – and they don't rhyme. For example,' he counted the syllables on his fingers.

'School's out for sum-mer
I could stay in bed all day
But I would get bored.'

He grinned. 'That's it. Short and sweet.'

'Can we sing?' asked Tomasz Kosecki.

'Well, as it's a *spoken word* competition, Tomasz, let's save singing for another occasion. But if you like, you can recite a song like you would a poem, or rap if you prefer – so long as you put your own spin on it.'

'When's the competition?' asked Callum.

'In a couple of weeks' time. I'd like to make a proper show of it and invite everyone's parents and carers. If

you don't want to perform, you could get involved in stage lighting, props or selling tickets. Ticket sales will go towards upgrading the school library.'

'Does the winner get a prize?' asked Callum, sounding like he expected to be the winner.

'A book token plus a serious dose of feel-good factor,' said Mr C.

Rom clenched my arm. 'Clem, you've got to enter – it's so you! Clem?'

I was frozen, my heart beating so loudly I imagined the entire class could hear it. An uncomfortable feeling of dread mixed with burning desire was coursing through my veins. What was wrong with me? I wanted to enter this competition with all my heart – and yet I was terrified that my performance would raise barely a half-hearted clap from the audience, yawns from the judges and a tonne of ridicule from Callum and my other classmates. There was no way I could put myself through that.

Out of the corner of my eye, I saw Callum leaning across the aisle towards me.

'Maybe you could enter a poem about Jammie Dodgers?' he smirked. 'Or Hobnobs? By the way, did you see they put my *winning* poem on the school website?'

I was about to give Callum a piece of my mind when Mr C caught my eye.

'Everything all right, Clementine?' he asked, frowning at me.

'Yes, sir.'

'You look a bit agitated.'

'I'm fine.'

'Would you like to enter the spoken word competition?'

'Er . . .' I scratched my ear. 'No thanks.'

'That's a shame. Still, you've got time to change your mind. I'll make a list of who's interested at the end of the week.' He turned his back to us and started writing the competition rules up on the whiteboard.

Rom turned towards me, confused. 'Why don't you want to enter? I don't get it – you *love* writing poems.'

I shrugged. 'Writing poetry is one thing – performing it out loud is another,' I said, then added for good measure, 'Anyway, *love*'s a bit of an exaggeration, Rom. I have other interests too, you know. And now I've offered to help look after Viv, I doubt I'll have the time. Scarlet macaws need a *lot* of attention.' I said this loudly, so that Callum would know my reason for not entering was nothing to do with him.

Rom turned away, unconvinced.

'What?' I asked.

'Well,' she said, turning back, 'if the school held a baking competition or an art competition and *I* said I wasn't going to enter, what would you say to me?'

Hmm, good point. I'd take her temperature and ask if she was feeling OK. But making multi-coloured show-stoppers or eye-catching papier-maché creations was Rom's speciality, and it would take someone pretty talented to beat her in a competition. Whenever she did enter a competition, she usually came in the top three. In other words, she didn't know what it felt like to lose, whereas I did. AND IT SUCKED.

'I'd say, just because you enjoy making stuff doesn't mean you should feel like you have to enter a stupid competition. Competitions aren't everything, you know?'

Rom pulled a face. 'Okaaaay, if you say so.'

'Yeah, if you say so,' echoed Callum, a stupid smirk on his face.

Clearly they didn't believe me. But if I tried any harder to convince them, I'd only make things worse. I needed to act like I didn't care one teeny weeny little bit. I needed to act like nothing Callum could say would bother me. In fact, what is it they say? *Attack is the best form of defence.*

99

Dad had told me he'd spoken to Neigh-Neigh last night and she'd been 'very understanding' about The Gum Incident, so I decided to take advantage of my little victory. I leant across the aisle towards him.

'Hey, Callum, are your trousers still sticky?' I teased. 'Did your mum get angry? Or did she see the funny side and have a good neigh?'

Callum's smirk vanished. HAH! I'd hit his weak spot. He scowled at the whiteboard before eventually answering back. 'And you think *your* dad's cool, do you?'

I hadn't really thought about it to be honest. No, he wasn't cool. He wore socks with sandals, sang really out of tune and let out monster burps when he thought no one was listening.

But at least he didn't have a laugh that sounded like a horse that had swallowed a helium balloon, which was a far worse crime against coolness in my opinion. However, I decided not to press the point.

Mr C clapped his hands. 'Right, has everybody taken note of the spoken word rules? Good.' He wiped the whiteboard clean and pressed a button on his laptop. A picture of an old white man smoking a cigar appeared on the wall.

'Time for some history.' Mr C perched on the end of his desk. 'Does anyone know who that is?'

Everyone stared blankly at the picture. Callum raised his hand and Mr C nodded at him.

'Is it Winston Churchill?'

'Correct. He took over as prime minister of Britain a year after the Second World War began. And can anyone tell me which countries were on which sides during the war?' I looked around the classroom. I knew that Britain and Germany had been enemies, but that was it.

Rom chewed her pen. 'I *so* know this!' she muttered. 'But I've forgotten.'

Callum put his hand up. 'Britain, France, America and Russia were on one side and Germany, Italy and Japan were on the other.'

'Excellent, Callum,' said Mr C. 'I'm impressed. Russia was known back then as the Soviet Union.'

Rom sighed. Callum tried to stifle a grin. *Gah! He was so annoying!*

'And both sides were doing a lot of spying on each other,' Mr C continued. 'Intel – meaning intelligence, or information – was key. Each side needed to know exactly what the other side was up to – what kind of weapons they

had, what information they knew, what their next move was, and so on. Both sides would even feed false information in order to outsmart the enemy.'

As Mr C carried on talking, certain words jumped out at me: *intel, false information, next move* . . . Suddenly, I had a brainwave – an utterly spy-tastic idea about how to get Callum and Neigh-Neigh out of my life.

CHAPTER 9

AN HOUR OR SO LATER

I DISCUSSED MY CUNNING MASTERPLAN WITH ROM OVER LUNCH IN THE HALL.

'I don't think that's a very good idea,' she said as we finished eating.

'Why not?' I said. 'I've got to do something! And anyway, you seemed quite happy about The Gum Incident making things awkward between my dad and his mum – which it didn't, by the way.'

'Yeah, but that was an accident,' said Rom. We got up and carried our empty plates over to the trolley. 'Now you're talking about doing things on purpose. That's different.

That could cause trouble!'

'Um, hello? That's the whole point!'

'Listen, Clem, my parents have always taught me and my sister that you should give people a chance. Get to know them a bit before you judge them. Look for the similarities and not the differences.' We headed out of the hall towards the playground.

'You're talking about being judged cos of your skin colour,' I said, remembering conversations we'd had about racism. 'But this is nothing to do with skin colour – it's totally different.'

'It may be nothing to do with skin colour, but are you sure it's so different? Have you forgotten Pippa Pig? And Moody McMoo-cow?'

Er, yes. I had forgotten. I hadn't thought about them in ages. Pippa Pig was someone who used to work with Dad. She wore a lot of pink, had very pink cheeks and always had her hair in pig-tails. And for a while she always seemed to be hanging around, smiling and giggling at all Dad's silly jokes. And Moody McMoo-cow was an old school friend of Dad's who hadn't stayed with us in ages but at one time seemed to visit a lot. She was the opposite of Pippa – super-serious and kind of grumpy. Pippa and Moody both seemed like ages ago and while I don't think either of them were like *proper* girlfriends, I'd been only too pleased when they'd stopped coming round.

'What about them?' I asked.

'Well maybe they were really nice and you never gave them a chance? A bit like you're doing now with Callum's mum, maybe?'

She left the question hanging in mid-air while I went to find Callum in the playground.

I was annoyed. If my plan had been a balloon, Rom had basically just gone and stuck a pin in it. Callum was a rude, mean-spirited, horrible person. If anything, he'd never given me a chance. I wasn't the one being unfair. And it wasn't like I *hated* Neigh-Neigh – she was a nice enough person, I just didn't want to be her step-daughter and have Callum for a step-brother. Was that so wrong of me? I don't think so!

I found Callum playing King's Squares with a bunch of others, so I hovered nearby until he got knocked out. This, I was pleased to notice, didn't take long and earned him a few boos (mainly from Luke McDonut, who had no respect for anyone who messed up with a ball).

He went to walk past me, but I stepped in front of him, blocking his path. 'I have an idea,' I announced.

'Bet that doesn't happen very often,' he snarked, trying to walk round me.

I blocked his way again, ignoring the sarcastic remark. 'You don't want your mum going out with my dad, and I don't want my dad going out with your mum, so I've come up with an idea.'

He stopped. 'Go on then, *Tangerine*. I'm listening.'

'They still don't know each other that well. So, I thought we could give them fake information about each other – things that would *put them off* each other. For example, my dad hates perfume and anything that smells perfumey, like scented candles and room sprays. So, if you tell your mum that you heard me say my dad *loves* perfumes, she'll put loads on and he'll be grossed out. Get it?'

Callum frowned at me. I wasn't sure whether he thought my idea was ridiculous, or whether he was too proud to admit that I was a total genius.

'Or how about . . .' I wracked my brain for another example. 'Like maybe your mum hates beards. So, I tell my dad your mum *loves* beards – like *big, bushy, Father Christmassy* beards – so he starts growing one to impress her, but it totally cringes her out. See?'

I waited for him to say something, but he just carried on

looking at me like I was a weirdo so in the end I gave a casual shrug and walked away. Clearly I was going to have to carry out this plan by myself.

'She doesn't mind beards,' he called out.

I turned round.

'But she hates it when men shape their eyebrows, or when they use too much stuff on their skin and hair.'

Bingo! Although, to be honest, I'd been hoping for something a little less complicated. The only way I'd be able to shape my dad's eyebrows was if he was asleep. And I'd probably have to use plasters or gaffer tape to strip off the hair. I imagined Dad waking up with a blood-curdling yell and throwing his mystery attacker across the room in shock.

'OK . . . Got any other ideas?'

'Not yet,' snapped Callum. 'Give us a chance!'

'All right, don't get your Y-fronts in a twist. Just find out what things annoy her. For example, my dad hates it when people post photos of their dinner on the internet – which is the kind of thing you could easily persuade your mum to do.'

Callum thought for a minute.

'She hates it when people say 'end of' instead of 'end of story'.'

107

I sighed.

'What?' he scowled.

'Well I can't exactly get my dad to start speaking differently, can I?'

'Have you tried?'

'Look, just try to find out some more things that annoy her and let me know. The main thing is: do you think that if we put our heads together we could somehow split them up?'

Callum pulled a face. 'Maybe.'

'I'll take that as a yes. Welcome to Operation Bad Romance.' I held out my hand to seal the deal, but he looked at me like I had a contagious disease and walked off.

Whatever.

'Maybe when we get our phones back at home time we should swap numbers?' I called after him. 'Send each other intel?'

I headed back to Rom as the bell sounded for end of lunch break.

'What did he say?' she asked as I caught up with her.

'Operation Bad Romance – or OBR for short – is go,' I said smugly.

She gave me the same kind of look my mum gives me when I fill my glass of orange juice right to the brim.

'Be careful, Clem.'

As I reached my front door, I could see Eddie Two-Balls sitting in Ingrid's window, waiting for her to get back from school. As soon as he saw me, he started barking excitedly and wagging his tail. I waved to him and let myself into my house.

Dad called out from his study. 'Hi Clem-cakes! Just finishing up some work. Be with you in a minute.'

'Where's Lottie?' I asked.

'On a play date.'

Good. That would give me an opportunity to fish for useful information. I slung my bag on the table, took a cup out of the cupboard and put the kettle on. *Hmm.* Even though I knew many of my dad's likes and dislikes when it came to everyday life, clearly I didn't know what he liked and disliked when it came to girlfriends. Who knew a laugh like a horse wouldn't bother him, when the sound of Lottie cracking her knuckles made him beg for mercy? I needed to find out what would bother him – and what would hopefully bother *her*.

'Is my kind, lovely daughter making me a cup of tea?' Dad called out from his study.

'Why, of course she is!' I replied, quickly grabbing another cup from the cupboard and bunging a teabag in it.

Dad walked into the kitchen, rubbing his eyes. 'I'm seeing double,' he yawned. 'Been staring at my screen all day trying to write a newsletter which basically has no news to go in it.'

I poured hot water into the cups and stirred the tea.

'Dad, name three things that make you *really* annoyed,' I said as casually as possible while getting the milk out of the fridge.

'Aside from writing newsletters with no news in them? And finding at least three dirty cups in your room every day?' He went to tickle me in the ribs but I dodged out the way.

'I don't mean things about work and family, I mean what things do you find annoying about *other* people?'

'OK . . . interesting question. Let me think . . .' He stroked his chin while I passed him a cup of tea. 'Nope. Can't think of anything. Why d'you ask anyway?'

I shrugged. 'No reason. I was just thinking about that TV programme you like – the one where the guests do a show-and-tell of things that really bug them.'

Dad chuckled. 'Oh, I see. You want to know what my *pet hates* are?'

'Yes!' *Pet hates*. That was exactly what I meant.

Dad slurped his tea. 'Let me think . . . When people drive right up close behind me. That winds me up a bit.'

A bit? Um, *a lot*, if you ask me. Anyway, as I couldn't exactly get Neigh-Neigh to follow him around in her car, this information was of no use whatsoever. *But they were bound to follow each other on Instagram or Facebook!*

'What about pet hates on social media?' I asked, pretending to be distracted by choosing a biscuit from the tin.

'Ooh, where to begin?' Dad rubbed his hands together enthusiastically. 'When people post photos of food – that annoys me. Or when they tag you to name your top ten favourite films or whatever – Angie Gordon was always doing that. It was when she tagged everyone to name their top ten favourite cookery books that I finally snapped. So I replied with my top ten favourite species of worm and she unfriended me. *Result!*' Dad punched the air.

I smiled as I imagined Neigh-Neigh tagging Dad to name his top ten favourite breakfast cereals.

'Also, when people post endless pictures of their pets or their babies or their five-star holiday in the Maldives –

oh, and don't even get me started on selfies!' Dad shook his head despairingly.

Brilliant – there was so much to choose from! I was certain we could use some of this.

'Political ranters, attention-seekers, people who—'

'Dad, OK!' I put my hand on his arm to calm him down.

'I've started, so I'll finish – people who say Pink Floyd's *Dark Side of the Moon* is overrated or 'Who likes U2 anyway?', like no one else's opinion matters.' Some spittle flew out of his mouth and landed on my cheek. *Yuk!* I wiped it away with my sleeve.

'Dad, maybe you should give up social media? I don't think it makes you very happy.'

Dad looked at me. 'You're absolutely right, Clementine.'

Oh no! What had I gone and said? He couldn't give it up *now*, when I needed Neigh-Neigh to go and do all the things he'd just mentioned.

'Or just cut down a bit.'

Dad nodded. 'Yes, well I've cut down a lot. You can see why I don't want you using social media just yet, can't you?'

I was pretty sure I wouldn't get as wound up about those kinds of things as Dad did. I *loved* pictures of yummy food,

cute pets and sandy beaches! I didn't mind other people's selfies and I would LOVE to share my top ten favourite films – or even my top ten favourite cereals! But my parents had agreed I wasn't allowed any social media accounts until at least Year Seven and, when my parents agreed on something, there was no point arguing (believe me, I'd tried. I'd also tried asking for a new phone but was told I'd have to make do with Dad's old one for the 'foreseeable future'). Luckily Rom's phone was as old as mine and she wasn't allowed on social media either, so at least I wasn't the only one.

'Are you popping over to see your feathery friend this evening?' asked Dad, draining the last of his tea and making a big show of putting his cup in the dishwasher.

'Dunno.' I needed to write down all his pet hates before I forgot them. And while I very much wanted to write a poem on Lyn's wall, I didn't have one that was good enough.

'And how's our local punk legend doing?' asked Dad. 'Still skating to the loo?'

Suddenly I remembered Lyn's question. 'She wanted to know which of her songs is your favourite?'

'"Educating Mr Martian",' Dad said without hesitation. 'It's about a teacher who's really an alien from Mars who doesn't understand the school rules, and the kids have

to teach him the rules so that he doesn't give himself away. It's brilliant cos it makes school rules sound really stupid.'

My eyes widened.

Dad started shouty-singing, playing air guitar and throwing his head back and forward like he was head-butting an invisible wall.

'Mr Martian, the thing with schools
Is that they have some stu-pid rules
And lots of point-less reg-u-lay-tions
That's just Brit-ish edu-cay-tion.'

Surely this song had something to do with Linda Jones's short story?

'Is Lyn Ferno her real name?' I asked.

'No,' laughed Dad. 'Her real name's Linda Jones. Her punk name is a play on the word *inferno*, which means an out-of-control fire. 'Educating Mr Martian' was her biggest hit from her punk era – it's on the *Black Eye* album. I'll dig it out, if you like?'

I pictured a young Linda Jones crying into her pillow, her story screwed up in the wastepaper bin, her confidence crushed. And then I pictured all the framed gold discs

hanging in her hallway – '. . . *in recognition of outstanding achievement and worldwide success*.'

'Maybe later.'

I bolted upstairs to get changed. I was going to see Lyn Ferno straight away. Suddenly I had a lot more questions to ask.

CHAPTER 10

FIFTEEN MINUTES LATER...

AFTER TEXTING CALLUM A LIST OF MY DAD'S PET HATES, I THREW ON MY RIPPED JEANS AND A LUMINOUS YELLOW T-SHIRT AND DASHED OVER TO LYN'S HOUSE. AS I ENTERED HER BEDROOM, I NOTICED LYN HAD A CAT-PATTERNED NIGHTIE ON THIS TIME. I WONDERED IF A CHANGE OF NIGHTIE MEANT SHE'D HAD A SHOWER?

'Look who's come to see you, Vivian!' cooed Lyn, putting her novel to one side and taking off her reading glasses. 'Call him,' she instructed me, patting her shoulder.

'STAND AND DELIVER!' I commanded and patted my

shoulder. Viv flew straight to my outstretched arm, greeting me with several bing bongs and a squawk.

'Hello, cuteness!' I said, nuzzling his head with my nose.

'So, did you ask your dad which of my songs he likes best?' asked Lyn, pinching her clumps of orange hair into spikes.

'He said 'Educating Mr Martian'.'

'Had a feeling he'd say that. Did the title sound familiar?'

'Did it come from your 'Teacher from Outer Space' story?'

Lyn chortled, revealing a set of wonky teeth that were more magnolia than her bedroom walls. 'It did indeed. Once thirteen-year-old me had had a good cry, I took it out of the bin, straightened out the crumples and put it in my drawer. Ten years later, I rewrote it as a song and, after performing it in a grotty hole in Croydon one night, I was offered a recording contract! So, tell me, Clementine, how do you feel about your poem now, the one you entered for that school competition?'

I shrugged. I still felt it wasn't very good. I wished I'd written something completely different – something grown-up and clever.

'Perhaps I could read it?' Lyn asked.

I didn't get it. Why was she so keen to see my poem?

It's not like my silly rhyme about custard creams was ever going to become a hit record. Lyn watched me while I dithered. I suppose it was nice that she was interested. Other than my mum and dad, no one had ever asked to read one of my poems before. And even though Lyn was nuttier than a nut festival in Nuttington County, lots and lots and *lots* of people – like my dad – thought she was a legend. And besides, I had a feeling she wasn't going to let it go.

'I can recite it if you want?' I said.

'Fabulous!' Lyn clapped her hands.

'*Bing bong!*' chirped Viv.

I ushered Viv up my arm and on to my shoulder and took a deep breath.

'"An Ode to Custard Creams' by Clementine Florentine – that's my nom de plume,' I added.

'I do not understand
The craze for mega cookies
Simple British biscuits ROCK
And shouldn't be overlookied.

Take the custard cream
A beige rectangle of magic

A cup of tea without one
Is sad and rather tragic.

The custard cream's a classic
There is no greater pleasure
Than dunking one in your tea
#NationalTreasure!'

'Clementine . . .' Lyn shook her head sorrowfully.

GAH! I knew she'd hate it! I wished I could rewind the clock to five minutes earlier and tell her I'd rather take my stupid poem to the grave than share it with anyone ever again.

'You see? I told you it wasn't very good,' I said defensively.

'*What?*' She frowned. 'I think it's fantastic! So what if it didn't win? That doesn't mean it's no good. I bet it took you a long time to write that.'

'It did. *A whole day*.'

'But I bet you enjoyed yourself writing it.'

I did. I *loved* writing poems.

'Listen here, *Clementine Florentine*, just because your poem didn't win the competition doesn't mean the judges didn't like it. Tastes can vary not just from one person to another, but from one year to another and even one *day* to another. For example, I usually have porridge for breakfast, but some mornings I fancy toast instead. I used to look down my nose at murder mysteries, but now I'm hooked on the flipping things.' She jerked her thumb at one of the novels on her bedside table. 'Anyway, I bet you the next time one of those judges eats a custard cream, they'll remember your poem and smile.'

I got what she was trying to say, but it didn't change the fact that my poem just wasn't as good as Callum's. And no adult trying to make me feel better was going to change my mind.

I took my phone out of my pocket, looked up the school website and found Callum's winning entry. 'Look – this is the poem that won the poetry competition last term.' I passed her my phone. 'It's not just *a bit* better than mine – *it's in a different league!*'

Lyn reached for her glasses and squinted at the screen. She cleared her throat.

'The Window by Callum Harvey.

I like the view from this window
It looks out on to a garden

Where people are laughing
Holding drinks with ice
A smell of sun cream and barbecues
Ollie, Spike, JJ and me
Kicking a ball around
Dripping with sweat
Mum says burgers are ready
Dad says come and get them
It tastes so good
Now the garden's empty
The leaves are turning brown
Everything's in boxes
It's time to leave
And I won't get to see this view
From this window
Ever again.'

She took her glasses off and passed the phone back to me.

'I like this too,' she said. 'A memory of a summer's day with his family and his friends – or perhaps they're his brothers? It sounds like he's moving house and he's going to miss that garden. I can really feel his sadness. Yes, moving house can be very sad . . .' Lyn's voice trailed off.

Feel his sadness?

I hadn't thought about it like that. I'd been too busy feeling jealous that his poem sounded more grown up than mine. I felt a twinge of pity for Callum, seeing as I knew what Lyn didn't – that it wasn't just his house and his friends he was missing, but his mum and dad being together, too. I didn't really remember what that felt like any more, as my parents had split up when I was six.

'Anyway, your poems are completely different,' said Lyn. 'You can't compare them, really. Maybe the judge was feeling a bit sad that day and Callum's poem struck a chord. A different judge on a different day may well have preferred yours.'

'But I wasn't even a runner-up!' I complained, the disappointment stinging all over again.

Lyn tutted. 'So are you just going to give up and never put your poems out there again?'

I avoided her gaze and kept my eyes fixed on Viv, stroking his feathers all the way down to their tips over and over again.

'I wouldn't have taken you for a quitter, Clementine.' Lyn threw back the duvet and swivelled round, her nightie riding up to reveal two hairy, veiny legs with stripy socks on

her feet. She slipped into her roller skates and reached for the rope. 'Need a wee,' she said, pulling herself towards the bathroom and shutting the door behind her.

I put Viv back on his perch while I let her words sink in. I hadn't quit *writing poems* – I'd just quit *entering competitions*. Not the same thing! Therefore, I wasn't a quitter. The bathroom door opened and Lyn rolled out, pulling herself back along the rope to her bed.

'You *mustn't* give up writing poems, Clementine,' she continued, easing herself back into bed and pulling the covers over her. 'Just because your poem doesn't win a competition doesn't mean *you're not talented*. We all take a kick in the gut occasionally, girl – it hurts. But then you get up, put your boxing gloves back on and get back in the ring.' She clenched her fists and jabbed the air. 'Hiding yourself away isn't the answer.'

As I imagined myself bouncing around a ring in enormous boxing gloves, Lyn wriggled down under the covers, pulling her fake fur blanket all the way up to her chin.

'Um,' I opened my mouth and closed it again.

'What? Spit it out, kid.'

'Well, aren't *you* hiding yourself away?'

Lyn blinked at me. 'This is just temporary.'

'Did *you* take a kick in the gut?'

She stared up at the ceiling and pursed her lips. I had a feeling I'd said the wrong thing and perhaps it was time I left. Just as I was weighing up the best way to make a hasty exit, she let out a loud sigh.

'Yes, I did take a kick in the gut. A big one.' She looked sad.

'What happened?' I asked.

She massaged her forehead. 'OK. Here's the deal. The next time you come, I'll tell you my story if you agree to write a brand-new poem on my wall.' She slipped a thin white arm out from under the covers and held her hand towards me. 'Deal?'

I still wasn't sure how I felt about writing a poem on her wall, but I was curious to know what had happened to her. So I stepped forward and shook her hand.

'Deal.'

CHAPTER 11

THAT SAME EVENING . . .

WHEN I GOT HOME FROM LYN'S, I WALKED INTO AN
EMPTY KITCHEN TO FIND A SAUCEPAN BUBBLING
AWAY ON THE STOVE. I LIFTED THE LID AND PEERED
INSIDE. DAD'S CHICKEN CASSEROLE. BLEURGH!

My phone beeped. It was a message from Callum.

Callum: Top ten – check. Selfie – check.

Me: Awesome! Easy.

Callum: NOT easy.

Me: How did you get her to do it?

Callum: Will explain at school.

Me: Did u find out what things annoy your mum?

I waited for a reply, but none came. Eventually I put my phone back in my pocket.

'Hello? Where is everyone?' I called out.

'In here!' Dad replied from his study.

'Where's Lottie?' I asked, leaning in his doorway.

'Upstairs firing arrows at her teddy bears.' He turned to look at me. 'Hopefully I'm nurturing the hobby of an Olympic archer and not a fledgling serial killer.'

'What are you doing?' I noticed he was looking at Facebook.

'Just working on my blog.'

'That's not your blog.'

Dad was about to click it away, but I grabbed his arm before he could move the mouse.

'Isn't that Mel?' I pointed to a pouty-lipped selfie of Neigh-Neigh that made her look prettier than she actually was.

'Yeah . . .' grinned Dad, leaning back in his twirly chair and folding his arms behind his head. 'Indeed, it is.'

'But she's doing a *duck face*,' I said.

'Uh-huh. . . What's a duck face?'

I pouted my lips, sucked in my cheeks and stuck my face in Dad's.

He shrank back. 'Oh, right.'

'I thought you hated selfies?' I frowned at him.

'Normally I do but as that's an undeniably nice photo of her, I'll make an exception in this case.'

I noticed he'd already clicked the like button. *For God's sake!*

'What else has she posted?' I asked.

'None of your business.' He clicked Facebook away and swivelled round to face me.

'I was just asking,' I said sullenly.

'If you must know, she's asked me to list my top ten favourite songs of all time.'

'A top ten? But you *hate* top tens!'

'True, Clem. But over the years I've asked myself this very question many, many times and quite frankly, it's time I worked out – once and for all – just *what are* . . . DA-DA-DAAAAH . . .' he played an imaginary organ, *'Raymond*

Norris's Desert Island Discs! It's making my brain ache! Oh, wait!' He slapped his forehead and pointed to the framed poster of Ziggy Starburst that hung above his desk. 'Nearly forgot the thin white duke himself – *what am I like?*' He returned to the keyboard, muttering to himself as he typed.

I walked out of his study in disgust. Neigh-Neigh had just committed two of Dad's biggest pet hates and got away with it. I was going to have to up my game.

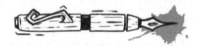

The next morning on the way to school, I checked my phone to see if Callum had replied yet. I'd waited all evening and not a word from him. RUDE!

'Um, hello? Are you listening to me?' Rom pulled a face.

'Sorry, what did you say?'

She rolled her eyes. 'I said, do you want to come for a sleepover this Saturday night? My mum says it's fine.'

'Oh yeah, cool – let me check with my dad.' I checked my phone again.

'Why do you keep looking at your phone?' she grumbled.

'I'm waiting for Callum to send me some intel. We need to take things to the next level.' I gave her the lowdown on

what happened last night, while looking out for Callum as we walked through the school gates.

'At this rate, you and Callum might actually end up being friends,' she said with a laugh.

'Don't be ridonculous,' I replied.

I spotted Luke McDonut showing off on the King's Squares pitch with a group of others but there was no sign of Callum. It turned out he was already in the classroom, sitting in his chair and looking at pictures of surfboards on his phone.

'Why didn't you text me back last night?' I hissed as me and Rom sat down.

'It took *time* to get the intel,' he hissed back, wary of Rom overhearing.

'Sounds like Operation Bad Romance hasn't got off to the greatest start,' said Rom, sounding like she wanted to add 'told you so'.

'You mean *she* knows?' Callum pointed at Rom. 'Who else have you told?'

'No one! You don't need to worry about Rom,' I said solemnly. 'She's been my best friend since reception.'

'You can trust me.' Rom crossed her heart. 'I swear.'

He looked at her doubtfully. 'Do NOT tell anyone else.'

'I won't. Haven't you told Luke McDonut?' asked Rom.

'Nope. Why would I tell him? Just because I play King's Squares with him occasionally doesn't mean he's my friend. Anyway,' Callum put his phone down, 'you should know it wasn't easy getting my mum to post things she wouldn't normally post.'

'So how did you get her to do it?' I asked.

'I said her hair looked really nice and she should post a selfie so your dad could see it. But she said she wouldn't want anyone thinking she was vain. So I said your dad didn't seem like a judgey kind of person – but if he *was* judgey, then maybe she shouldn't be his friend in the first place.'

I smarted at the word 'judgey'. I didn't like people thinking badly of my dad. However, I suppose judgey was exactly what I needed Dad to be right now.

'OK, gimme some solid intel on your mum,' I said. 'Quick – I can hear Mr C in the corridor!'

'Man, *chill*,' groaned Callum. 'She hates sport and fitness and gets annoyed when people go on about how quickly they can do the park run. Her worst nightmare would be running a marathon.'

She sounded annoyingly similar to Dad.

'Oh, and something else. She doesn't like it when men

wear too much make-up.'

'*Okaay* . . .' And what was I supposed to do with that information exactly? Get my dad to start wearing make-up? Was Callum mad? I tried not to laugh.

'What's so funny?' Callum glared at me. 'Loads of men wear make-up! It's the 21st Century – not Victorian times, you peanut-brain.'

Rom placed a hand on my arm. 'Maybe you should hear him out?'

'I'm all ears!' I sniggered.

'My mum and Uncle Leo had a row once when she told him he wore way too much blusher and eyeliner for a guy, which Uncle Leo said was sexist. She told him that apart from Captain Jack Sparrow, most men look silly in make-up. That's not my opinion by the way, I'm just passing on intel.'

'Who's Captain Jack Sparrow?' I asked as Luke threw himself on the chair next to Callum, panting and sweating.

'From *Pirates of the Caribbean*,' said Rom.

'Oh.' A film I'd wanted to watch when I was about five but Dad reckoned it was too scary for me at the time – a wrong that needed to be put right ASAP.

'He's a pirate with long hair and jewellery and lots of eye

make-up,' said Rom.

'*What?* You haven't seen *Pirates of the Caribbean?*' sneered Luke, still catching his breath.

'Shut up, sewage breath!' I shot back as Mr C entered the classroom and folded his arms. We all fell silent.

'Good morning, everyone!' boomed Mr C.

'Good morning, Mr C!' we boomed back.

Mr C went through the register while I sighed inwardly at the thought of the task that lay ahead. Get Dad into sport? No chance! Get him to wear make-up? *Gimme a break.*

I was so busy thinking about Operation Bad Romance when I got home from school that day that I didn't notice Ingrid calling me from the other side of the street as I searched for my keys in my school bag.

'Coo-eee! Wait up, chicken!' She had her hair in side-plaits and was wearing a bright red, flowy dress with Eddie Two-Balls in a matching lead. Eddie dragged Ingrid across the road towards me, like the world's strongest man pulling a tractor.

'How's you, Clementine?' she asked as Eddie dropped

both his balls at my feet and jumped up at me, his tail wagging at fifty miles per hour. 'Eddie, get down!' snapped Ingrid. 'Got food on you?'

'A half-eaten banana,' I replied. (It was Rom's. She was waiting for the right time to tell her mum she'd gone off bananas. In the meantime, she was giving them to me).

'That'll be it, then. Greedy mutt. Anyway, Clementine, I've got a favour to ask—' She stopped and frowned at me. 'You look troubled. Is something bothering you?'

I couldn't exactly tell Ingrid that I needed to find an easier way to get my dad to break up with Neigh-Neigh, but I *could* ask her if she had any bright ideas on how to get Dad to take up a sport. It was worth a try.

'Well, it's just that . . .' I paused to gather my thoughts. 'Do you know how I can get my dad to do more sport and exercise? He's nearly forty-five, so time is running out.'

Ingrid smiled. 'Ah, bless you, Clem. You don't need to worry about him, he looks pretty fit and healthy to me.'

'No, he's not! He spends all day sitting at his computer. He needs to start running or something!'

'Well, you can't force anyone to exercise, sweetie – they have to want to do it for themselves. But you could suggest you start getting fit *as a family*. In fact, the favour I wanted

to ask of you was whether you could you look after Eddie this Saturday? Maybe you could take him for a run round the park? He'll get you all fit, for sure.'

RESULT OF RESULTS!

I could just picture me, Dad and Lottie jogging round the park with Eddie Two-Balls trotting alongside us. I could suggest we time ourselves and then get Dad to post the results on Facebook. Easy! A few gentle reminders that he wasn't getting any younger and I'd have Dad signing up to do a half marathon in no time at all.

'I'd love to look after Eddie!' I said. 'I'll check with my dad. Can I ask you something else, Ingrid?'

'Fire away, chicken licken!'

'Do you think men should wear make-up?'

Ingrid leant towards me. 'Personally, I think there's nothing cuter than a man in guyliner – like his royal purpleness, Prince, or a young Simon Le Bon . . .' Her face went all dreamy. 'Right.' She gave her head a brisk shake. 'Come on Mr Two-Balls! Time to go home and search for that missing money again.'

'Missing money?' I echoed.

'Yes, it's a mystery. I left a twenty-pound note on my coffee table and then it was gone – unless I'm getting the

days mixed up and I actually spent it, in which case I'm losing my flippin' marbles. Anyway, don't forget to mention Saturday to your dad. Ta-daah, babes!'

I waved goodbye, let myself in and came under immediate attack from Lottie and her bow and arrow.

'NOT NOW!' I shouted. 'Where's Dad?'

'Upstairs. How about a pillow fight then?'

'Later.'

I got myself a cup of tea and sat down at the table with my phone.

'What are you doing?' asked Lottie, sliding into the chair next to me and tilting my phone towards her.

'Looking up Captain Jack Sparrow.'

'Hey, Clem.' Dad walked into the kitchen. 'What d'you think of this shirt?'

It was the same as all his other shirts. 'Meh,' I said, barely looking up.

'Damn,' he sighed. 'You're right. I've invited Mel over for dinner tomorrow night and I could do with a shirt that isn't *meh*.'

Dinner? I sat up straight. *Tomorrow night? So soon?*

'Is Callum coming?' My shoulders stiffened.

'No, he's seeing his dad tomorrow night, so you can

relax – it's just Mel.'

Thank God for that. I leant back in my chair.

'And don't worry, you don't have to eat the same as us – unless you fancy aubergine curry?'

'Aubergine?' Lottie made a puking sound.

'It's a recipe Rom's mum gave me,' said Dad. 'And it's totes delish-balls. But clearly your tastebuds aren't *mature* enough yet. Anyway, back to my shirt . . .'

'Your clothes are BORING,' said Lottie. 'You only wear dark blue.'

'Yes, thanks, Lottie. I'm fully aware I need to branch out a bit.'

'I could style you if you like?' she said. 'I'm good with clothes.'

Suddenly a golden opportunity seemed to be shining right in front of me. 'Why don't you let me and Lottie give you a makeover?' I said.

Lottie leapt up from her chair. 'YES!' She ran over to Dad and squeezed him tight. 'We'll make you look handsome so Mel will want to marry you!'

Pass me a sick bucket! Clearly my sister and I were coming at this from different angles. At some point we needed to have a serious chat – but not yet. If anything, right now she

was making my challenge a lot easier.

'Why not give your mum a makeover the next time you stay with *her*?' Dad backed away from us. 'And Lottie, no one's getting married, OK?' He glanced at me nervously.

'Oh.' Lottie stuck out her lower lip. 'But if you do, can me and Clem be bridesmaids?'

GAAAAH! Someone shut this maniac up!

'Girls, listen. As I already said to Clem, Mel and I are just getting to know each other. We're not boyfriend and girlfriend. Not yet, anyway.' Dad took a deep breath. 'So, Foghorn doesn't mind Mel coming round tomorrow night – does that go for you too, Clem?'

I hesitated. Did I tell him the truth – that I very much *did* mind? Or did I stick to the plan I'd persuaded Callum to go along with? I reckoned if I told Dad exactly how I felt about Mel – that she was fake, her laugh was embarrassing and her son was a major moron – it's not like he'd say, 'OK, Clem, I'll stop seeing her if it makes you happy'. No. I was smart enough to know that wasn't going to happen. All I could do was act cheerful and hope that mine and Callum's meddling would eventually make them realise they were better off as just friends. (Friends who didn't need to see each other very often).

'Clem?' Dad nudged me. 'Are you OK about Mel coming tomorrow night?'

It was time to play *hardball*. 'Only if you let me do your hair and make-up.'

'Another time, Clem – not tomorrow night.'

'Why? Are you worried she'll be judgey?' I said, remembering how Callum had got Mel to post her selfie. 'Cos if she's a judgey person, then . . . ' I pulled a face.

'She's not judgey!' Dad laughed. 'OK, hair possibly – NOT make-up.'

Lottie got down on the floor and knelt in front of Dad, her hands pressed together in prayer. 'PLEEEEEASE!'

'Hair definitely AND make-up definitely,' I bargained hard. 'Anyway, I happen to know that Mel has a major crush on Captain Jack Sparrow.'

'Good grief!' Dad guffawed. 'We're having a curry at home, not going to a fancy-dress party!'

'That's not what I meant,' I said angrily. 'What I mean is that she likes men who wear make-up.'

'And how would you know, Detective Shermadge?' He obviously didn't believe me.

'Cos Callum told me.'

'So, if you and Callum are talking to each other, does that

mean you're getting on a bit better now?'

'Sort of. Anyway, it's not just Mel – Ingrid likes men who wear make-up, too. Just now she went all swoony over the Purple Prince Le Bon.'

'You mean Prince?' Dad seemed confused. 'And possibly Simon Le Bon?'

'That's it – and Prince is into purple make-up.'

I wasn't sure who any of these people were, but Dad seemed surprised and thoughtful, as if maybe what I was saying wasn't so ridiculous after all.

Lottie got up off the floor. 'So, do you want to look *meh*? Or . . .' She looked to me for help.

'Or do you want to look . . . *miaaaaow*?' I said, waggling my eyebrows and making claws with my fingers.

Dad held up his hands in defeat. 'OK, OK. If that's what it takes to make you two happy, knock yourselves out. Lord have mercy.' Dad grabbed an orange from the fruit bowl and disappeared back upstairs, unbuttoning his shirt as he went.

'Bagsy I do his nails,' said Lottie.

I took an orange out of the fruit bowl and smiled to myself. I'd just had a GENIUS idea – if I did say so myself.

'And bagsy,' I sniffed the orange, 'I do skincare.'

CHAPTER 12

THURSDAY

THE FOLLOWING EVENING, AFTER WOLFING DOWN OUR TEA, ME AND LOTTIE SPREAD OUR LOTIONS, POTIONS AND MAKE-UP NEATLY ACROSS THE KITCHEN TABLE, READY FOR DAD'S MAKEOVER.

Dad brought his laptop so he could read the news while Lottie sat opposite him, painting each of his finger nails a different colour. I stood on his other side, holding a tube of leftover self-tanning cream that, along with all my other make-up, I'd persuaded Mum to give to me ages ago. I squirted a blob on to my fingertips and massaged it into his cheeks and forehead, before applying another layer.

Feeling doubtful that this stuff actually worked (I'd only tried it once and probably hadn't used enough), I applied one more layer for good measure.

'What *is* that stuff?' Dad asked me. 'It's a bit pongy.'

'Just moisturiser,' I said, chucking the now-empty tube in the bin. 'And it's not as pongy as your aubergine curry.'

'My curry smells like it tastes: *Delicious*,' he said proudly.

Dad had spent *two hours* making a curry, trying to get the flavour just right, as Neigh-Neigh had warned him she didn't like food that was too spicy – a golden piece of intel that Dad had given away all by himself. A piece of intel that would be *rude* to waste . . . 'STOP FIDGETING!' shouted Lottie. 'You made me go wrong.'

Dad examined his multi-coloured nails. 'Mel's gonna think I'm weird,' he sighed.

'You ARE weird,' said Lottie.

'Seriously, Dad! I told you already – she's going to love it,' I lied, stretching his eyelid towards me while I applied the black eyeliner I'd borrowed from Rom.

'*Sweet cheeses, merlot and jalapenos*!' yelled Dad, batting my hand away. 'That HURT!'

'Stop whining,' I said, painting a cute little Ariana Grande-style flick on the far corner of his eyelid.

'Whoa! I think that's a step too far.'

'DAD!' I stamped my foot and pointed towards the poster in his study. 'Imagine if Ziggy Starburst was standing here right now – what would he say to you?'

'He'd say his name is *David Bowie* and that Ziggy Star*dust* was his one-time stage name. Have I taught you nothing?'

'I'm being serious.' I folded my arms.

Dad thought for a minute. 'He'd say, 'For heaven's sake, Raymond. What happened to you? You used to wear eyeliner back in the day. When did you become such a boring old fart?''

He nodded for us to continue and I dabbed some pink lip gloss on his lips while Lottie grabbed a tuft of his hair and yanked it into a mini-ponytail.

'OW – CAREFUL!' growled Dad, his eyes watering. 'I can't take this abuse much longer.'

'Nearly finished,' said Lottie, sprinkling a small bottle of sparkly fairy dust on top of his head before holding up a mirror for him to see what he looked like.

'*Oh. My. God.*' Dad's eyes bulged. 'What have you done to me?'

Mission accomplished: Dad looked like he was about

to star in a Christmas pantomime. No self-respecting adult would want to hang out with him looking like *that*.

Lottie pouted. 'We made you look pretty! You ought to pay us really.'

The doorbell rang and he stood up. 'OK, that'll be Mel. Time to clear this stuff away and get ready for bed.'

'You're not allowed to wipe it off,' I said.

'Wouldn't dream of it,' Dad muttered, heading for the front door.

Time for part two of my evening's goals: *kill that romantic dinner*.

I accidentally-on-purpose knocked Lottie's fairy dust on to the floor. 'You dropped something,' I said. As soon as she crawled under the table, I grabbed the jar of chilli powder from next to the stove and emptied it into the steaming pot.

'Need a hand with all those nail varnishes?' I asked, quickly putting the jar back as she stood up again.

'OK.'

Laughter came from the hallway and we stopped to listen.

'Yeah, so forgive me for looking like a cross between Robert Smith and Tinkerbell,' said Dad.

There was a snorty sound, followed by: 'Actually, I think

you look quite sexy like that,' followed by some serious neighing.

YUCK! DISGUSTING! WASH YOUR MOUTH OUT, LADY!

I turned to Lottie with my vomit face, but she was doing a stupid happy dance with imaginary pom-poms. I rolled my eyes.

Was Neigh-Neigh for real? She couldn't really mean what she said about Dad looking 's' (I couldn't bring myself to say the word). Surely she was just being polite. She couldn't exactly say, 'Wow, you look ridiculous', could she?

We trooped out of the kitchen carrying our nail varnishes and eye pencils and were hit by the smell of perfume. Poooeeee! Neigh-Neigh smelt like the perfume counter in Boots. I resisted the urge to pinch my nose. I wondered how Dad was managing to breathe.

'Girls!' boomed Neigh-Neigh. 'So lovely to see you!'

'Hi, Mel!' chirped Lottie. 'Do you like Dad's makeover?'

'I love it, Lottie!' she replied. 'You'll have to do me next time! And how are you, Clem?'

'Good,' I mumbled and quickly carried on up the stairs, desperate to escape the perfume cloud before I choked to death.

'Good night, you two,' said Dad, showing Neigh-Neigh

into the kitchen. 'I'll come up and check on you later, although I'm *sure* you'll both be fast asleep.'

I pulled my bedroom door shut behind me and flopped on to my bed. All that effort to make Dad look cringe and Neigh-Neigh *loved* it.

However, the game wasn't over yet.

I changed into my jimble-jambles and got into bed with my poem book. While waiting to hear screams of horror from either A) Dad turning orange, or B) super-spicy curry being eaten, I busied myself with writing a poem for Lyn's wall.

I thought autumn would be a good theme, because the excitement I'd felt at starting Year Six and being in Mr C's class was wearing off fast. I hated our stupid tomato-coloured school jumpers. I hated singing stupid childish songs in assembly. And more than anything, I hated getting up early. I wished I could just hibernate in my bed until spring. Just roll myself up like a sausage in my duvet and stay there where it was warm and cosy.

A while later, I heard someone creeping up the stairs.

'Dad?' I called softly.

Neigh-Neigh poked her head round my bedroom door. 'Only me, I'm afraid. Just popping to the loo. Do you need something, sweetie?'

Sweetie? *Bluurgh!*

'No. I mean, yes.' Might as well ask her, seeing as she was here and I was stuck with my poem. 'What rhymes with *duvet*?'

'Gosh,' said Neigh-Neigh. 'That's a challenging question. Er . . .' She scratched her head. 'I know – *Vouvray!*'

'What's Vouvray?' I asked.

'Fizzy bubbles. You know – for special occasions? Excuse me, Clem, I must dash to the loo, I've been guzzling water.'

'Why?' I sat up in bed. 'Didn't you like the curry?'

'Oh no, the curry was *amazing. So* cinnamony – which is odd because I never told your Dad I like it cinnamony, but he totally smashed it.'

What was she on about? How could they not taste all the chilli powder I tipped in?

'So, it didn't taste too spicy?'

'Not at all. Must dash – I'm bursting. Night, night, Clem.'

It's Clementine to you, you silly old horse – not Clem. ROAAAARR! I imagined the look on her face when she discovered there was no loo roll, as it may have 'accidentally' rolled under the bath and out of sight.

I jotted down the word Vouvray and put my poem book away. I was starting to feel sleepy, but I needed to stay awake to find out if Dad was turning orange.

The next thing I knew, the sun was streaming through my curtains and Dad was sitting on the end of my bed dressed in a suit. I blinked myself awake.

WHAT THE FANGTASTICS?!

I sat bolt upright and stared at my Dad's bright orange face. He was holding something in each hand. I rubbed my eyes and forced them to focus.

'Are we awake yet?' asked Dad. 'Because I have a few questions for you.'

I blinked at him and grunted, blinded by the orange glow coming from his face. That stuff SO worked!

He held up a jar of cinnamon. 'This was practically a full jar when I was cooking last night,' he said. 'But when I next looked at it, it was almost empty. Care to explain?'

I pulled my most innocent face. 'I don't know what you're talking about.' Which was kind of true, seeing as I was as confused as he was. I never touched that jar. I touched the *chilli jar*. So, yes – I needed an explanation, too.

'Really, Clementine? Please don't insult my intelligence.

A jar of cinnamon doesn't just pick itself up and pour itself into a curry.'

'Have you asked Lottie?' I said. 'She *so* wanted you and Mel to have a perfect evening, maybe she thought she was making your curry extra tasty? And from what I heard, Mel loved it.'

'True, she did,' said Dad. 'Although I'm not convinced my smash-hit curry was created by an act of love rather than an act of *sabotage*.'

'Why not?' I shrugged.

'Because of this.' He pointed to his orange face. 'And this.' He held up the empty tube of Bronze Goddess Self-Tanning Creme.

I tried to disguise a giggle with a cough.

'I wondered why Mel kept asking if I was feeling OK last night. She said I looked a little off-colour, like I could be coming down with something. It wasn't until I saw myself in the bathroom mirror just now that I realised 'off-colour' is putting it mildly.'

'*Oops*,' I said. 'I think I may have used a bit too much.'

'*Really?*' said Dad sarcastically. '*You don't say?*'

'I didn't mean to!' I looked offended. 'I didn't realise how strong it was!'

Dad held my gaze for a while. 'I've got a lunch meeting with my boss today. I've got important things I need to say to her – like asking for a pay rise, making much-needed changes to the newsletter and being allowed to continue working from home – things I need her to take seriously, which she's unlikely to do while I look like Donald Trump after five cans of Fanta.'

I gulped and looked down. 'I'm sorry, I didn't read the instructions properly,' I lied, feeling majorly guilty and stupid.

Dad sighed. 'OK. I'll give you the benefit of the doubt just this once, but take note, Clementine – I've got my eye on you.' He stood up and headed out of my room, keeping his eyes on me all the way.

CHAPTER 13

JUST OVER AN HOUR LATER

'SO,' SAID MR C, LEANING AGAINST HIS DESK AND HOLDING UP THE PIECE OF PAPER THAT HAD BEEN STUCK TO THE DOOR ALL WEEK, 'IS THERE ANYONE ELSE WHO WANTS TO SIGN UP FOR THE SPOKEN WORD COMPETITION?' HE GLANCED AROUND THE CLASSROOM.

Rom nudged me. '*Go on!*' she whispered.

'*Sssh!*' I whispered back, not wanting to draw attention to myself.

'But you could win this time!'

I ignored her. I didn't want to ignore her, but Mr C was

looking right at me with raised eyebrows.

'Anyone?' he repeated. I lowered my eyes. 'OK, great. That works out at about ten acts in total. Should be a good night, by the sound of it. I'll be sending an email out this evening inviting all your folks, but in the meantime, you might want to pencil next Friday 14th in your diaries – which is a bit sooner that I'd envisaged, but the only date that works in our insanely busy school calendar.'

The bell sounded for lunch break and Mr C dismissed us from the classroom.

'By the way,' I said to Rom. 'I asked Dad if I can come to yours for a sleepover on Saturday and he said yes.'

'Cool! But Clem, I can't believe you're not going to enter the spoken word competition.' Rom gave me a concerned look as we walked towards the canteen. 'You can't let what happened last time put you off.'

'It's nothing to do with *that*!' I said. 'I already told you. Too busy. No can do.'

I noticed Callum walking behind us, smirking.

'You could write a poem about a girl called Tangerine whose dad is a giant orange,' he said, overtaking us and joining the back of the lunch queue. I instantly regretted the update I'd sent him after finishing Dad's makeover.

'Or I could write a poem about a boy whose mum was doing so much neighing last night she went *hoarse*,' I replied. '*HOARSE* – get it?'

'Hilarious,' snapped Callum. 'You're so funny, I'm cracking up.'

'Yeah, well, your intel has been totally rubbish so far, you slimy green *snotberg*, and Operation Bad Romance is achieving the TOTAL OPPOSITE of what it's supposed to achieve.'

'*My* intel's rubbish? What about *yours*?'

'At least I've been trying!' I protested. 'Working out how to turn my dad orange without him knowing was pretty genius – and is more than you've come up with so far – and it's not my fault if your mum *still* finds him s . . . s . . .' I couldn't bring myself to say the 's' word.

'Sexy,' Rom giggled.

'Yes, *that*. Ugh!' I grimaced.

Callum's jaw clenched. He seemed to find the 's' word even more horrifying than I did. Was that because he still believed his parents would get back together?

'Does your dad have a girlfriend?' I asked him.

'Why? What's it to you?' He looked at me suspiciously.

'Well, it's just that my parents split up years ago so I

know they're not getting back together.'

Callum stared at the floor. 'He did have one but now he doesn't. It might not look like it to you, but my parents still love each other. They're just separating for a while . . . It's temporary.' His eyes turned watery and he blinked furiously, turning away from us and pretending he had something in his eye.

Rom and I glanced at each other. 'You mean,' said Rom, 'they're separating for a while to work out if they're, like, better off together or apart?'

'Something like that,' he said, over his shoulder. He sniffed a few times before turning round again, his face back under control.

I guess it must have taken some effort to reel those tears back into his tear ducts. If it had been me, I probably wouldn't have been able to hold back. I felt sorry for him and if he *had* cried, I wouldn't have given him a hard time. In fact, I would've liked him more.

'So maybe there's a chance they *could* get back together?' I said, trying to sound encouraging. 'Just not straight away.'

'But if they both get a new partner in the meantime, it'll *never* happen,' he said angrily. 'So, you need to start giving me some *proper* intel, Tangerine. I told my mum to put perfume on last night – which she did – and, when she wasn't looking, I sprayed it all over her coat and handbag too. She stank! But apparently your dad said she smelt amazing. So *that* was a waste of time!'

WHOA! Sympathy over. And to think I almost liked him for a few seconds!

'Well, I turned my dad into a glow-in-the-dark freak show and your mum STILL fancied him, so *that* was a waste of time, too!' I retorted.

'Guys!' said Rom. 'Stop arguing. What if your parents *really are* a good match for each other?'

'How would you know?' grunted Callum as we shuffled along in the queue towards the front of the canteen.

'Well, when my parents married, both their families were against it,' said Rom. 'My dad's parents wanted him to marry an Indian girl, and my mum's parents wanted her to marry an Italian boy. But they got married anyway and eventually everyone realised that my mum and dad were made for each other. And when me and my sister were born, it brought the two sides of our family even closer together. So, you know, maybe you should like . . . give your parents a chance.'

Even though she was my best friend, The Sensible One

could sometimes be really annoying. Talk of marriage and babies was the opposite of what me and Callum needed to hear right now.

'My mum and dad were meant for each other,' said Callum. 'Not my mum and *her* dad.'

'Yeah, thanks, but no thanks,' I said to Rom. I stepped closer to Callum and steered him to one side. 'Look, if we want to split them up, we need to come up with better ideas. For example, this Saturday, we're taking Ingrid's dog Eddie to the park, so I'll persuade my dad it's time for us to get fit so that I can turn him into the type of fitness freak your mum hates.'

'What if he doesn't want to get fit?' asked Callum.

'Oh, he will,' I said. 'Just leave it to me.'

I'd already thought of a simple but cunning plan.

After I got home from school, I got changed and went to see Lyn and Viv, hurrying down our road as it started to pour with rain. As soon as I walked into Lyn's bedroom, I noticed that NEIGH and POEM had now been joined by a floor-to-ceiling cartoon of a flamingo who looked pretty uninspired by its surroundings. Above its head was the word *'BOF'*.

'Is it raining outside?' asked Lyn, whose spiky hair was starting to look more grey than orange.

'Yes,' I replied. 'What does *bof* mean?'

'It's how the French say *pfff*.' She made a sound like a deflated balloon with an expression to match.

'Oh, you mean like *meh*?'

'In this instance, yes, precisely.'

'Did Pascal draw it?' I asked, coaxing Viv on to my shoulder.

'He's a cartoonist in his spare time. Not bad, is it?'

'*Bing bong!*' said Viv.

'I can't bear the suspense any longer,' said Lyn. 'Do you have a poem for me?'

I nodded. I'd worked on it before and after school, although I'd formed most of it in my head last night while Dad and Neigh-Neigh were having dinner. I pulled the piece of paper from my jeans pocket, unfolded it and handed it to her.

'NO!' Lyn backed away from me as if I was giving her a bottle of poison. 'I don't want to see it until it's up *there*.' She pointed to the wall.

'But . . .' What if she didn't like it? I wrote it pretty quickly. It seriously wasn't that good. I mean, it was OK, but I wasn't sure that it was ready to be put somewhere so . . . *permanent*.

'But nothing!' scoffed Lyn. 'Have some courage, Clementine. It's a poem – there is no right and wrong!'

'But I haven't spent much time on it,' I said. 'It's a bit rough still.'

'Even better. I prefer things that are a bit rough around the edges.' She nodded at the marker on her bedside table.

I picked it up and studied my scrawly handwriting on the piece of paper. Despite all her encouragement, I was pretty certain she was going to be disappointed. I unscrewed the lid on the marker and, holding my poem in one hand, pressed the pen nib against the wall with the other.

'Make it big enough for me to read from here,' she instructed.

I tried to make my handwriting as neat as possible, but, despite my best efforts, each line looked like it was sliding down a hill. When I finished, I stood out of the way, but kept my back to Lyn, afraid to see her expression.

She coughed. 'Autumn Schmautumn – by? You haven't written your nom de plume. Do that in a minute.'

Fun time's over, it's back to school
I'm gutted it's no longer summer
Wearing school uniform so isn't cool
Autumn is such a big bummer

As usual in autumn I catch a big cold
And sneeze like a snot-filled volcano
Who cares if the leaves are pretty and gold?
Dad tells me not to complain-o.

I switch on the heating – Dad says NO WAY
So I make a cocoon with my duvet
I'm not coming out till it's April or May
When I'll celebrate spring with some Vouvray.

Lyn slapped the mattress with both hands and let out a loud cackle. My heart started pounding.

'I love it!'

Yeah, right. So why are you laughing at me? I wasn't stupid. I could tell when an adult was softening a blow.

'*Bing bong! Bing bong! Bing bong! SQUAWK!*' shrieked Viv, joining in the excitement.

'Although,' chuckled Lyn, 'I'm not sure someone your

age should be drinking Vouvray.'

What was she on about? 'You don't *drink* Vouvray – you put it in the bath,' I explained. I suspected it'd been a very long time since Lyn had last had a bath.

She cackled again. 'There may well be such a thing as Vouvray bubble bath, but it's also a type of wine.'

I tried to recall Neigh-Neigh's exact words: *fizzy bubbles for special occasions.* She meant wine? Great. Nice of her to say so. Why had I even bothered asking her – let alone used her pathetic answer?

'Oh,' I said, my cheeks starting to glow. I knew this was a mistake. I put the marker back on her bedside table and placed Viv back on his perch.

'You need to put your name next to it,' said Lyn, popping a handful of mint humbugs in her mouth and making her cheeks bulge like a hamster.

'Doesn't matter,' I mumbled, heading towards the door.

'It absolutely does matter!' she said gruffly, picking up the pen and throwing it to me. 'Catch!' I caught it.

Now I felt like I was being bossed around and I wanted to leave – immediately. I quickly scrawled my name next to my poem and screwed the lid back on the marker.

'Your poem is a breath of fresh air, Clementine – just

like you! Stop thinking your poems aren't good enough and stop comparing yourself to others. Be yourself and stuff what anyone else thinks.'

As I put the marker back on her bedside table, she caught my arm and held it. 'It takes courage to be yourself, Clementine,' she said, looking into my eyes. 'But when you dare to show what you really think and feel, good things can happen.' Then she gave my arm a friendly squeeze and released me.

'I always write silly, childish rhyming poems,' I mumbled. 'I can't do serious ones like Callum.'

'Your poems are not silly or childish – they're *fun*. They're entertaining. There's no rule that says poems have to be serious, Clementine. Poetry is everywhere – it takes so many forms that we don't even notice we're reading or listening to poetry half the time. It's in TV commercials, radio jingles, children's books, political speeches, plays – hell, every pop song ever written is just poetry set to music!'

Gosh. How had I not realised this before? Was she right? Was poetry *everywhere*? From now on I'd be looking out for it, to see if it was true. Still, that didn't change the fact that my poems simply weren't very good.

'But Callum's type of poem seems to . . . to . . .' I couldn't put into words what I meant.

'You think his type of poem gets taken more seriously?'

'*Totally*.'

Lyn pondered for a moment. 'I suppose people under-estimate the importance of humour, Clementine, but where would we be without it, eh? How good do you feel when you're having a fall-on-the-floor belly laugh? Imagine a world without things that make you laugh – no funny TV shows, no funny books and *no funny poems*? It would be a pretty depressing place. Laughter keeps us sane. It's the best medicine – there's no truer statement.'

I looked at my poem on the wall. It had made Lyn laugh. That's what it was supposed to do!

'Thanks to you, I've rediscovered *my* sense of humour,' said Lyn. 'I thought it had died.'

'Punk is dead!' chirped Viv.

'Yes, I know.' Lyn smiled sadly at Viv.

'Why does Viv say that?' I asked. '*Punk is dead* – what does it mean?'

'My husband taught him to say it. It was our little joke.'

'*Your husband?*' I did a double take. I couldn't imagine Lyn with a husband, sharing a 'little joke'. I glanced around the room for signs of her husband's existence, but there were no pictures in frames. In fact, apart from the bed, the perch, the Union Jack throne-chair, Lyn's roller skates and a stack of books on the bedside table, there was nothing else in the room.

Lyn took a deep breath. 'Well, I did promise that if you wrote a poem on my wall I'd tell you my story. So, I s'pose I'd better keep my word.'

CHAPTER 14

A MINT HUMBUG OR TWO LATER . . .

AS SOON AS I SAT DOWN IN THE UNION JACK THRONE-CHAIR, VIV FLEW FROM HIS PERCH ON TO THE ARMREST BESIDE ME. I PLAYED WITH HIM WHILE LYN VISITED THE BATHROOM ON HER ROLLER SKATES.

'Where were we?' she said, returning to her bed, kicking her skates off and climbing back beneath the covers.

'Your husband?' I said, stroking Viv's head.

'My beloved Graham.' Lyn closed her eyes as if lost in a dream. 'We met about a year after I gave up my music career. I made some silly choices when I was younger, Clementine –

success went to my head. My comeback album in the mid-eighties did pretty well and I made a lot of money, but I lived a very unhealthy lifestyle and didn't look after myself at all. I got so depressed and ill that my sister, Cath – bless her – took me to a special clinic where you live for a while to work through your problems and become healthy again. I had a choice: 1) Get my act together with Cath's support, or B) Lose everything – including what was left of my mind. I chose A – she saved me.'

I gulped.

Lyn's eyes welled up and she gestured to the bathroom. 'Some bog roll, if you'd be so kind.' I hopped off the chair and went into her en suite where I noticed a Mickey Mouse toothbrush by the sink and another stack of paperbacks on a little table next to the loo. As I settled back into the armchair she gave her nose a good blow, making the loudest trumpety sound I'd ever heard.

'Gordon Bennett!' squawked Viv, practically jumping out of his feathers.

'Anyway, I decided I couldn't live the rock 'n' roll lifestyle any more. So I bought a little house in the country and took up horse riding as a hobby. I'd always loved horses. And that's where I met Graham. He was the local vet. Met him

one day when he was treating a cow in a neighbouring field. He looked at me as I rode past on my horse and said, 'I'm a huge fan of yours – saw you and the Banshees play in '77 before you were famous.' Not only was he getting me mixed up with another singer, Clementine, but he was also standing in the middle of a giant cow pat which made me laugh so much I nearly fell off my horse.'

She blew her nose again, examined the tissue and pulled a face. 'Snot. Where does it all come from, eh? Anyway, where was I?'

'Graham thought you were someone else,' I said.

'Ah, yes. He was so embarrassed when I told him who I was, he asked if he could take me out for dinner to apologise. The rest is history. We fell in love, got married and set up an animal sanctuary in the countryside. We had cats, dogs, my wonderful horse Charlie, a ferret and then this crazy bird arrived one day.' She nodded towards Viv. 'We always tried to rehome the animals – but this gorgeous creature here, rescued from some idiot exotic animal smuggler – was so adorable we kept him. I named him Vivian after a character from one of my favourite TV shows – a *funny TV show* as it happens.' She gave me a meaningful look. 'I just loved that show, it made me howl with laughter – so, you

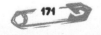

see, Clementine, who knows how your funny poems might inspire people?' I smiled and tickled Viv's head.

'But back to my story. Graham taught Viv to say 'punk is dead' because my record company kept pestering me to make a new album, but I had no desire to do that. I'd never been happier, living my simple little life in the country.'

Lyn paused, and her eyes drifted into the distance. I tried to picture her on her horse, or in her animal sanctuary, or with her husband Graham. It was strange to think of her being up and about, living a normal life. Something must have gone badly wrong.

'A few years ago, it all went belly up,' she said, her eyes fixed on her lap. 'Graham got sick and had to take this awful medicine which made him feel even worse than he did already. Meanwhile, Cath and I fell out when I had a row with her new partner, Helen. Helen and I didn't get along – stupid things were said and we just couldn't seem to resolve it. They moved to Australia and we've barely spoken since. The following year, Graham, my beloved husband and soulmate, started to fade away. I nursed him night and day and was with him at the end. I'm just grateful to have had him in my life for as long as I did.' Tears rolled down Lyn's cheeks. 'Cath wanted to come and visit but I told her I didn't want to see her. Stupid of me, I know. I had an opportunity to mend things but instead I made them ten times worse.'

My eyes went all blurry and I realised tears were rolling down my cheeks, too.

'When Charlie, my darling horse, died, I decided it was time to move house – I couldn't stay there, surrounded by memories. I settled on Brighton cos I've always been fond of the place – fresh sea air, fish 'n' chips, plenty of oddballs like myself. But a week or so after I moved in to this place, I woke up one day, and I just couldn't face getting out of bed.'

'How did you meet Pascal?' I asked.

'I put the word out I was looking for an assistant, and he got in touch. He's the son of an old friend of mine, and he's been a godsend – despite the fancy food choices and obsession with flamingos.'

'But what about your friends?' I asked. 'Surely you've got some friends who could come and visit?'

'Yes, yes, yes,' said Lyn with an irritable wave of her hand. 'But friends are always dropping dead when you reach my age. I can't face much more of that at the moment, so I'm happy to go it alone for a while. Besides, I'm not *completely*

alone – Pascal's on speed dial if I need him and Viv never shuts up, so you don't need to worry about me.'

'But don't you get bored?' I asked.

Lyn gestured to the stack of novels on her bedside table, and the multi-coloured pens and note pads scattered on her bed. 'Not really.'

'And don't you miss writing songs?'

'I've never stopped writing songs!' said Lyn, shocked by my question. 'I just don't *perform* them any more.'

'Why not?'

'Who wants to hear from a wrinkly old punk whose rock 'n' roll lifestyle consists of a snuggly duvet, a good book and a hot cup of tea?'

'My dad would.'

Lyn smiled.

'Don't you at least want to go to the beach? After all, you moved here to live by the sea.'

'The beach isn't going anywhere, Clementine. And I'm not in the mood right now to be hassled by well-meaning fans. I'm taking a break from the world until I feel good and ready to go outside again – which isn't yet. Not by a long chalk. Anyway, that's quite enough about me for one day. Will you write me another poem? I so enjoyed that one.'

'There's a competition coming up at school.' The words escaped from my mouth before I could stop them. 'A spoken word competition.'

'Is there indeed?' Lyn beamed. 'Well, Clementine Florentine, I sincerely hope you're planning on entering?'

I bit my lip and stroked Viv's wings. Maybe I would. *Maybe*.

CHAPTER 15

SATURDAY

STRAIGHT AFTER BREAKFAST, I'D GONE AND FOUND THE PHOTOS OF DAD FROM HIS STUDENT DAYS AND SPREAD THEM ACROSS THE KITCHEN TABLE.

One quick reminder of how he used to look many years ago was all it took to get him to agree to jog two laps of the park before having a picnic. While I was busy making sandwiches, he was upstairs trying to find something comfortable to jog in.

Suddenly, a terrified Fred rocketed into the kitchen and squeezed awkwardly through his cat flap to the safety of our small garden. Two seconds later, an over-excited Eddie Two-Balls came bounding in, stuck his head out the cat flap and barked at Fred.

'No, Eddie!' Lottie grabbed him by the collar and pulled him away from the back door. 'You mustn't frighten Fred.'

'Where are his tennis balls?' I asked. Ingrid had warned us how miserable Eddie got when he couldn't find his tennis balls. She'd also warned us to keep an eye out for picnics as Eddie was very greedy (though I doubted he could be any greedier than Fred).

'I hid them in the cupboard under the sink,' said Lottie. 'We're playing hide-the-balls. Did you know he can actually fit *three* in his mouth? We should rename him Eddie Three-Balls. Um, who's that salad for?' She grimaced at the plastic container I was pouring lettuce and tomatoes into.

'It's for Dad. He doesn't want sandwiches.'

'Why not?'

'He's on a diet.'

'Why?'

'Because he was looking at some old photos of himself, and they made him want to lose weight and get fit.' I really did have some genius brainwaves if I did say so myself.

'C'mon, Dad!' I hollered upstairs. 'Let's go! Lottie, go

and put your trainers on!' Why did I always have to organise everyone?

Lottie scampered back upstairs while Dad burst into the kitchen in a track suit and trainers, did a star jump, spun round and flexed his not-very-muscly muscles.

'Is that new?' I asked.

'No, it's just never been worn. And it's a little tighter than when I bought it.' He bent over to touch his toes and did a few stretches. 'Oh, by the way, Mel and Callum are joining us.'

WHAT? That wasn't part of the plan!

Dad saw my expression. 'What's the matter? You said you and Callum were on speaking terms now, so I thought you'd be OK with it?'

'But this is a *family* day,' I shouted. 'You didn't warn me there'd be *other people*!'

'I don't mind!' shouted Lottie from upstairs.

'Well, I DO mind!'

'I'm sorry.' Dad came towards me. 'You're right. I should've checked with you guys first. That was silly of me. I apologise.'

I breathed heavily, my chest inflating with anger.

'It's just that I texted Mel to say I was going jogging

for the first time in twenty years and she said she'd been meaning to start exercising, too. So I invited them along.'

What in the name of chocolate cheesecake was the point in running round the park now? It was all going wrong.

'Come on, Clem!' Dad gave me a playful punch on the arm. 'The more, the merrier, yeah? It'll be fun – all five of us running around with Eddie. Who knows – we might even manage to do five whole kilometres! And maybe we can get an ice cream on our way back?'

No amount of ice cream bribery could make this OK. I pulled a super-scowly face and shoved all the picnic stuff into Dad's rucksack as Lottie thundered back downstairs wailing.

'What's the matter?' asked Dad.

'Mr Miyagi's dead!' she howled. 'He's DEAD!'

'Oh, Lottie.' He gave her a hug.

'It's all my fault – I forgot to feed him! I *killed* him!'

Despite feeling sad about Mr Miyagi, without warning and for reasons I cannot explain, I exploded with laughter. It was totally unintentional. Like unexpected wind, it just popped out.

'Why are you laughing?' Lottie yelled at me.

'I'm sorry, I can't help it.'

'Shut up, Clem!' said Dad. 'You didn't kill him, Lots. Goldfish just don't live as long as humans.' He hugged her to him, stroking her head and comforting her. 'Mr Miyagi had a good innings, and I think he really appreciated that big tank we bought him on eBay.'

'Can we bury him at sea?' she sniffed. 'Near the pier?'

'If you do that, he'll probably just get washed up on the beach and eaten by a seagull,' I said.

'Not helpful, Clementine.' Dad eyeballed me. 'Um, here . . .' He handed Lottie the new beeswax wrap Rom's mum had bought for us. 'Go and wrap him in this and put him in the freezer. We'll take him to the beach for a proper funeral later.'

All this fuss over a goldfish!

While Lottie was fetching Mr Miyagi, Eddie brushed against my legs and pawed at the cupboard under the sink. I opened the cupboard and bent down to give him his balls back.

'Dad, can you think of a song we can sing at Mr Miyagi's funeral later?' asked Lottie, returning with a white parcel in her cupped palms.

Dad scratched his head. 'Er . . . hmm . . . How about . . . 'Candle in the Wind'?'

'How does it go?'

'Er, give me a sec. Maybe we should alter the words . . . ?'
Dad cleared his throat and sang in a deep voice.

'Goodbye Miyagi-san
Though I never knew you that well
I hope that you enjoyed yourself
With your treasure chest and shells

You were such a legend
Never once gave up exploring
Never once complaining
That your life was very boring

And it seems to me you lived your life
like a goldfish in a bowl
Never knowing where to swim to
in a world so small
And I wish I could've foreseen
how much my heart would ache
When your candle burned out long before
your bumper pack of flakes.'

Lottie walked at snail's pace towards the freezer as Dad

sang. Luckily, the doorbell went before the giggles took hold of me again.

'That'll be Mel and Callum,' said Dad, going to answer the door and nearly tripping over Eddie.

I stiffened as Neigh-Neigh and a grumpy-looking Callum walked into the kitchen.

'We're nearly ready,' said Dad.

At the sight of Eddie, a smile spread across Callum's face and he bent down to ruffle his ears. I was surprised at how different he looked when his lips pointed upwards – for a tiny second, I forgot how much I loathed him. And then the moment passed.

Chuffed with all the attention he was getting, Eddie turned towards Neigh-Neigh for more petting.

'Is that *your* dog?' she asked, edging away from him.

'No,' said Dad. 'Eddie belongs to our neighbour, Ingrid. We're looking after him for the day.'

'Mum doesn't like dogs,' said Callum. *Typical*.

'Oh, he's harmless,' said Dad. 'Go on, Mel, give him a stroke.'

'Do you like horses?' I blurted. 'I bet horses are your favourite animal.' I could tell Callum was glaring at me, but I pretended not to notice.

Neigh-Neigh gave me a baffled look and shrugged. 'Horses are OK, I suppose . . .?'

'Go on, Mum,' Callum urged her. 'He won't bite.'

She nervously reached forward to pat Eddie on the head, got a slobbery lick for her trouble and snatched her hand away, grimacing. 'I'll just go and wash my hands,' she said, swinging her backpack on to the kitchen counter and trotting upstairs.

'He's just being friendly,' I called after her.

'Unlike you,' Callum muttered under his breath.

'*Excuse me?*' I said.

'Come on,' said Dad. 'Let's wait for Mel outside. We can start warming up.'

Lottie and Callum followed Dad out the front door while I dashed to the freezer and quickly removed Mr Miyagi from the beeswax wrap. Before I could talk myself out of it, I unzipped Neigh-Neigh's bag, shoved him inside and zipped it back up as her footsteps came back downstairs.

'What on earth?' Neigh-Neigh halted in the kitchen doorway.

'What?' I froze, my heart pounding. Had she seen me?

'I think we should call a vet.'

It was a bit late for that. 'What do you mean?' I played dumb.

She pointed behind me.

I spun round. Eddie was lying spread-eagled on the floor, surrounded by cat biscuits and making a whimpering sound. I swooped towards him. 'Eddie! What happened?'

The cupboard door was open and Fred's giant bag of biscuits was spilling out, a large gash down one side. Neigh-Neigh ran to get Dad.

'Holy shenanigans!' gasped Dad, as everyone stampeded back into the kitchen. He yanked his phone out of his pocket and started scrolling desperately till he found the number he was looking for. 'Hello? My cat Fred Norris is registered with you – yes, Big Fred, that's the one – yes, he's sticking to his diet – I'm actually looking after a friend's dog and we've got an emergency . . . yes . . . well, he seems to have eaten himself into oblivion. I don't know – a huge sack of cat kibble, unopened till about five minutes ago . . . OK, we'll bring that too . . .' Dad put his phone away.

'NOOO!' wailed Lottie. 'It's happening all over again!'

'What is?' chorused Neigh-Neigh and Callum.

'Um, regrettably Mr Miyagi passed away this morning,' said Dad, scooping up Eddie in his arms. 'But if we hurry, Eddie will be fine, so keep it together, Lottie. Right, who's coming with me to the vet's?'

'Me,' said me and Lottie.

'Um . . .' Neigh-Neigh looked very much like she'd rather go home. 'Well, if you, er, feel you need some moral support?' She was clearly hoping he didn't.

'That's very kind, Mel' said Dad. 'I really appreciate it. Let's go everyone!'

Callum rolled his eyes.

Fifteen minutes later we were at the vet's where Eddie was laid on the table and given an injection. The vet, super-strict Sandra (every treat-loving cat's worst nightmare), chatted merrily to him as she pulled out the needle. Lottie winced and closed her eyes. *Some warrior woman.*

'If you wouldn't mind placing the kibble on the pet scales?' Sandra nodded to Callum who heaved the giant sack on to the large metal rectangle.

Lottie and I frowned at each other. Why did she want to weigh the sack of biscuits?

'That's a 12kg sack, isn't it?' she said. 'How much does it weigh now?'

'Nine kilos,' Dad replied, just as Eddie barfed all over the table.

'And there's your missing three,' tutted Sandra.

'GROSS!' groaned Callum, covering his nose and inching away from the mountain of stinky brown sludge on the table.

'Shut up! It's not Eddie's fault,' I snapped.

Neigh-Neigh gagged and turned to face the window.

'I'm not blaming him,' said Callum.

'Then keep your opinions to yourself!' I said. 'And you gagging and turning your back on him isn't exactly offering moral support either!' I barked at Neigh-Neigh.

'Clementine – *enough!*' Dad placed a firm hand on my shoulder. 'Mind your manners.'

'Anyway . . .' interrupted super-strict Sandra, 'if you hadn't found him when you did, it could've been curtains. He's basically just eaten a week's worth of food in one day.'

We all cringed. When Ingrid had warned us that Eddie was greedy, I'd just thought she meant he wouldn't turn down a biscuit. I mean, does *anyone* turn down a biscuit? But this gave a whole new meaning to the word.

'Smells really fishy in here,' said Lottie through her pinched nose. 'It's making my tummy feel funny.'

'Yes, I've been smelling fish ever since we left your place,' agreed Neigh-Neigh.

'Probably because they're salmon-flavoured biscuits,' shrugged Dad.

'Right, well, take him home and let him rest,' said Sandra. 'And for goodness' sake, keep your kibble somewhere out of reach.' She raised a stern eyebrow.

As we got back in the car, I demanded that Eddie sit on my lap rather than go in the boot. Dad looked unsure. 'I think the boot's the best place for him right now, Clem.'

'He's whimpering – he needs comforting!' I pleaded.

'If he pukes near me, I'll puke too,' warned Lottie.

'It's not like there's anything left in him to puke out!' I argued.

'I'll have him on my lap in the front if you like,' said Neigh-Neigh, surprising us all – including herself, by the sound of it. She was obviously trying to suck up to me and Dad after being so useless at the vet's.

'Well, that's very kind of you, Mel. Are you sure?' said Dad.

'Like Clem said, his stomach's probably empty.'

'Happy, Clem?' asked Dad.

'Fine,' I said begrudgingly.

We all got into the car and set off for home, the smell of fish growing stronger by the minute.

Dad tried to get through the traffic lights before they turned red, but didn't make it in time. We stopped, and then it happened: a loud gurgly noise followed by a smell that would've been toe-curling enough in the open air (let alone trapped inside a small car) followed by a blood-curdling scream. Eddie had pooed on Neigh-Neigh.

Screaming and gagging, we all wound down our windows at lightning speed.

'*Not happening,*' squeaked Neigh-Neigh, shaking in her seat and looking like she was about to throw up.

Dad gulped. 'You can do this, Mel,' he said, clenching the steering wheel with one hand and her quivering shoulder with the other. 'Everyone, stay calm. It's just poo – not bubonic plague.'

I leant forward to check out the crime scene: wobbling like a jelly on Neigh-Neigh's trembling lap sat a large Mr Whippy-shaped poo with something poking out of it – a bit like a soggy, purple Flake.

'DAD!' I yelled. 'LOOK! TWENTY QUID!' It had to be Ingrid's missing money. The mystery was solved AND she'd get her money back. She'd be so pleased!

'I NEED TO GET OUT!' shrieked Neigh-Neigh, sending Eddie hurtling into the back and on to my lap.

'Calm down, Mum,' groaned Callum, his T-shirt pulled up over his nose.

Finally, the lights turned green, and Dad sped round the corner and pulled up outside a petrol station. Neigh-Neigh leapt out squealing and hopping from one foot to the other as Eddie's 'mess' fell from her lap and splatted on to the ground.

One by one we tumbled out of the car, gasping for air. Dad handed Neigh-Neigh a wadge of serviettes from the glove compartment while I pulled a tissue from my pocket and carefully extracted Ingrid's £20 note. Dad then bagged up Eddie's squidgy poo as best he could.

'That's disgusting,' grumbled Callum. 'I wouldn't touch it if I were you.'

'Well you're *not* me, Wimpfred Von Wimpleton.'

'It's my fault,' said Dad. 'I should've put him in the boot *like my instincts were telling me to*.' He scowled at me.

'Why are you looking at *me*?' I snapped. 'I offered to have him on *my* lap – I never said he should go on *her* lap. She doesn't even like dogs!'

'Look!' said Lottie, pointing to a pressure hose on the far side of the petrol station. 'Maybe we could hose Mel down?'

190

I giggle-snorted.

'I'm failing to see the funny side right now, to be honest,' snapped Neigh-Neigh, shooting me a dirty look as she chucked the soiled tissues in a nearby bin.

'So am I,' said Dad. 'Just zip it, Clementine.'

'It wasn't *my* idea to invite Callum and Neigh-Neigh!' I shouted. 'It was supposed to be a *family day* – remember?'

Everyone stared at me.

'WHAT?' I yelled.

Wait – did I just call her Neigh-Neigh out loud?

Oops!

CHAPTER 16

A FIFTY-THREE-MINUTE ETERNITY LATER

I SAT ON MY BED, MY POEM BOOK RESTING ON MY LAP. WORDS WERE COMING AT ME LIKE A TIDAL WAVE, BUT I COULDN'T SEEM TO GET THEM IN THE RIGHT ORDER. FOR THE FIRST TIME EVER, THEY WERE DARK, ANGRY SENTENCES, JUMBLED UP LIKE A NEST OF SNAKES ALL BITING AND SNAPPING AT THE THOUGHT OF NEIGH-NEIGH AND CALLUM RUINING OUR FAMILY DAY.

Neither Dad nor Lottie said a word to me after we dropped Neigh-Neigh and Callum off, but I knew Dad was waiting till we got home and then it was just a matter of time before I was in for it.

I heard the front door bang downstairs. He was back from taking Eddie home to Ingrid. Two seconds later there was a loud knock on my door and Dad barged in, without waiting for permission. I snapped my poem book shut and slid it under my duvet. I wondered if Neigh-Neigh had found Mr Miyagi yet and grassed me up?

'Your behaviour today was UNACCEPTABLE!' he shouted. 'What gives you the right to speak to Mel like that? What has she ever done to you?' He towered over me, huffing and puffing, his face as red as a tomato. I kept quiet, knowing that to defend myself would only make things worse. 'You didn't even have the decency to apologise when I asked you to. I'm *so* embarrassed – that's not how Mum and I brought you up. I've texted Giulia to say you're not going for a sleepover tonight. You're grounded.'

NO! That was SO unfair! Not only was I desperate to pour my heart out to Rom, but what would her mum think of me now?

'It was supposed to be *just the three of us*,' I shouted. '*The three of us and Eddie.*'

'I already apologised for that,' Dad shouted back. 'Sometimes plans change at the last minute – that's life.

You need to be able to adapt and put a smile on your face, even when you don't feel like it. It's not a reason to be mean to people.'

Tears pricked at my eyes and, before I could stop them, rolled down my cheeks, splashing on to my duvet.

Dad sighed and plonked himself down on the end of my bed. We sat in silence for a few minutes before he eventually asked, 'Is Callum still being mean to you?'

'We don't get on – just like you and Uncle Robert don't get on.'

Dad considered this for a bit. It was no secret he'd never liked Mum's brother.

'The person who said Dark Floyd's *Pink Side of the Moon* is overrated and 'Who likes 2U anyway?' – that was Uncle Robert wasn't it?' I said. 'And even though you haven't seen him in ages, you *still* call him Southern Fried Plankton.'

Dad's lips twitched. 'That's because he always used to call me Northern Monkey Boy.' He sighed. 'OK, fair enough, so you don't get on with Callum – but what about Mel? I can't understand why you don't like her – she's been nothing but nice to you.'

I hugged my knees to my chest and hid my face. *I just didn't like her*. And I didn't like sharing Dad with her.

I liked it when it was just the three of us. But it felt petty and childish to admit that to him. I knew I wasn't being fair and yet there was an achey feeling of sadness inside me that I couldn't explain.

'I mean, you seem to get on OK with Mum's boyfriend,' he said. 'So I don't understand what the problem is – apart from you're not a fan of Callum.'

'Is Mel your girlfriend now?' I asked.

'No, but what if she becomes my girlfriend? You'd have to find a way to get on with her. And you and Callum would have to find a way to get on with each other. I know it's a new situation for you, and that it'll take some getting used to, but if you give Mel and Callum a chance, get to know them better, you might enjoy their company as much as you do Simon's.'

'So, she basically *is* your girlfriend then!' I shouted.

Dad didn't answer immediately. 'It's looking like a possibility, Clementine – well, if she still wants to see me after today.'

I burst into tears. Dad tried to put his arm round me, but I shook him off.

'Clem,' he pleaded. 'I love you and Lottie more than anyone in the world. Nothing will ever change that. Mel

wouldn't dream of coming between us. *She's a nice person.* I'm sorry I invited her and Callum along without warning today. Next time I'll consult with you and Lottie first.'

'Lottie wants you and Mel to get together because she wants to wear a bridesmaid's dress and scatter petals.'

Dad rolled his eyes. 'We're a very, *very* long way from that scenario. I don't even know if I want to get married again.'

'But if she becomes your girlfriend, won't we all have to live together – in the same house?'

'Clementine, I don't even know if we'll be dating in a month's time – like I keep saying to you, we're still getting to know each other and that takes time. It might turn out we're not compatible after all. It might turn out we are. I don't have a crystal ball, so can you allow me the chance to find out?'

I wondered if we could order a crystal ball from Amazon. It would come in *very* handy.

Dad pulled me towards him for a hug and I hugged him back. I hated it when we argued.

'I promise to give you more notice in future when I'm thinking of inviting Mel and Callum. But can you promise to give Mel a fair chance, please?'

I nodded. It was an auto-nod, rather than a promise, because I didn't want Dad to be angry with me any more.

'Be kind to people,' said Dad, kissing me on the forehead. 'And kindness will come back to you.'

This made sense. I hadn't been very kind at all and I was now slightly regretting slipping Mr Miyagi into Neigh-Neigh's rucksack. This would be the last straw. When Dad found out he would sell me on eBay to the lowest bidder – if there were any bidders.

'Dad . . .' I took a deep breath. Time to fess up.

'Yes?'

Then I remembered the anger in Neigh-Neigh's voice when she'd said she was failing to see the funny side – a comment that was meant for me and me alone. She obviously didn't like me any more than I liked her.

'What is it, Clem?' he said.

'Nothing.'

'DAD!' Lottie's voice screeched up the stairs. 'COME HERE, NOW!'

Dad sighed, heaved himself off my bed and trotted downstairs.

I had a feeling my dastardly deed had just been discovered and, as it was likely my phone would be confiscated within the next five minutes, I quickly texted Rom to say I was sorry I couldn't come over. She messaged back immediately.

Rom: I don't understand. What happened?

Me: Dad thinks I was rude to Neigh-Neigh. Which I sort of was.

Rom: 😠 😾 I think you should stop Operation Bad Romance before you get in even bigger trouble.

Me: What?! No way! 😦

Rom: Is Neigh-Neigh really that bad?

Me: Er hello?? I thought you were on my side? 😲

Rom: I am!

Me: 💀

I waited for Rom to pledge her loyalty, but no reply came. Surely she could see it wasn't *my* fault I'd been grounded? If anything, it was *Neigh-Neigh's* fault! I felt hurt by her silence. What kind of friend was Rom if she didn't support me when I needed her most?

'Clementine!' shouted Dad. 'Can you come here, please?'

I composed myself and made my way downstairs to where Dad and a sobbing Lottie were standing next to the freezer, the empty beeswax wrap laid out on the side – its contents gone.

'It would seem,' said Dad calmly, 'that Mr Miyagi was more special than we ever knew.'

'Special?' I asked. 'What do you mean?'

'Well,' he said, winking at me while Lottie buried her head in his belly, 'like Jesus, he seems to have risen from the dead, discarded his shroud and left his resting place. Pray tell, Clementine, has he appeared to you in a dazzling white light and given you any celestial advice?'

Was this a trick? What was I supposed to say?

'What does celestial mean?'

'Heavenly.'

'Um . . . yes?'

'Tell us what he said then!'

'He said . . .' I wracked my brain. 'He said it was a bit chilly in the freezer so he was going to heaven now, and could we all please remember to be kind to one another.'

Dad gave me a secret thumbs up and patted Lottie's back.

'He also said,' I continued, 'that everyone makes mistakes

and should be given a second chance. And that if Clementine seems like she's making a lot of mistakes right now, to go easy on her, because she's only ten and she's still learning.'

'Oh per-leeease!' groaned Lottie. 'He did NOT say that.'

'Lottie, go and choose a film for us all to watch,' said Dad. 'We need some chill time. We've had enough drama for one day.'

'Can we watch *Moana*?' she asked.

'OK,' said Dad. 'You go and set it up, me and Clem will join you in a sec.'

As soon as Lottie was out of the room, Dad closed the door and raised his eyebrows at me.

'*What have you done with him?*' he whispered.

'It was an accident,' I whispered back. 'I went to see if he'd frozen yet but I dropped him on the floor and accidentally broke him, so I put him in the bin, but by then he was in two different pieces so it might be tricky to find him in there.'

Dad leant closer to me. 'It's just that a very fishy smell seemed to follow us everywhere this afternoon, Clementine, suggesting that Mr Miyagi's body was with us as much as his soul.'

'You said yourself it was the salmon-flavoured biscuits.

If you don't believe me, go and rummage in the bin.'

Dad glanced at the bin. 'Tempting. I'll take your word for it, BUT . . . if I find out you're lying, your phone will be confiscated – FOR GOOD.'

I inhaled. 'Can we go and watch *Moana* now?' (Words I never thought I'd say).

He gave me a lingering suspicious look, before opening the kitchen door. I walked swiftly into the living room and leapt on to the sofa. Dad followed me and settled between us, his arms spread round our shoulders.

The three of us. Just how I liked it. Even if I did have to sit through *Moana* again.

My phone buzzed.

Callum! What did that slimy snot-rag want now?

'Who are you texting?' asked Dad.

'Just Rom,' I said.

He yawned, put his feet up on the coffee table, leant back and shut his eyes.

I flicked my phone on silent and, shielding it from Dad, opened up Callum's message.

Callum: My mum found a dead fish in her bag.
Any ideas how it got there?

Me: Probably Eddie.

Callum: There's only one place Eddie would put a dead fish and that's in his stomach.

Me: What did your mum say?

Callum: She knows this situation is hard for me and you, so she's not telling your dad – this time.

Me: OBR is going nowhere and you are NOT helping.

Callum: Actually, Tangerine, you're wrong. Make sure your dad checks Facebook before it's too late. #Skillz

Dad had almost nodded off when his phone buzzed. Opening his eyes, he leant forward, picked it up off the coffee table and clicked on a notification, keeping it tilted away from me. I pretended to be watching *Moana*.

Out of the corner of my eye, I sensed Dad's face harden. He sat up straight, scrolling on his phone. Something was up. He opened his mouth to say something, then closed it again.

'Are you OK?' I asked.

'What?' he huffed. 'Yes, fine.'

'*Ssssh!*' hissed Lottie, turning the volume up.

'*What the . . .?*' Dad stared at his phone in disbelief.

'*What?*' Lottie and I chorused, staring at him.

Dad shook his head, chucked his phone back on the coffee table, rubbed his tired eyes and sighed heavily.

'*DAD! What?*' I pressed him.

'Nothing, nothing. Just remembered I need to send a work email. I'll do it from my computer so as not to disturb you guys. Back in five minutes.' He got up and disappeared into his study.

The second he was out of the room, I grabbed his phone before the screen locked.

'What are you doing?' asked Lottie, dragging her eyes away from the TV.

'Just admiring Dad's phone,' I lied. 'It's so cool. I want one like this.'

She turned back to *Moana*, mouthing the words to 'You're Welcome'.

I glanced at the phone screen – the Facebook app was open. Underneath the name Mel Harvey was a selfie of Neigh-Neigh and a friend looking a bit bedraggled and pulling stupid faces. I scrolled down. Mel Harvey had also posted three pictures of fluffy kittens with the caption, 'LOLZ', a picture of a giant chocolate cake saying, 'NOM NOMZ' and a picture of Captain Jack Sparrow that said, 'SUPER CRUSH'.

Finally, Callum had made himself useful.

I opened the notification Dad had just received: it said that Mel Harvey had changed her relationship status. Unsure what that meant, I clicked on the word *About*, and found myself reading a list of things about Neigh-Neigh. Apparently she worked for Brighton and Hove Council and was . . . *MARRIED TO RAYMOND NORRIS!*

HOLY ARCTIC ROLLY! (As Dad would say).

As much as I hated Callum, I had to admire his nerve. This was a supremely gutsy move – not that I would ever tell him that, as he was too big for his boots already. I carefully placed the phone back on the table.

Was this the reason Dad was looking grumpy and stressed? Had Neigh-Neigh's posts on Facebook wound him up? Had he seen the bit that said they were married? He must have! I had a good feeling about this. If my instincts were right, Dad was finally thinking it was time to say night-night to Neigh-Neigh.

I closed my eyes and prayed.

CHAPTER 17

SUNDAY

THE FOLLOWING DAY, DAD SUGGESTED I PAY LYN AND VIV A VISIT. I KNEW THAT LYN WOULD ASK ME IF I HAD A NEW POEM FOR HER, SO I TOOK MY BOOK WITH ME.

Last night, I'd filled pages and pages with poems – some short and silly, some long and angry. I crossed most of them out. I just needed to let the words out, higgledy-piggledy, until there were no words left to come. It felt a bit like deflating an airbed when you lie on top of it, pull the stopper out and feel yourself sink to the ground as the air comes whooshing out.

Eventually I'd started to feel a bit better and was able to write something I felt almost proud of.

When I got to Lyn's, Pascal opened the door and let me in.

'Clementine!' He greeted me with a big grin. 'Oh, thank goodness you're here. Maybe she will listen to you.'

'About what?' I asked.

'This crazy bed-in. It is bad for her health.' He leant closer to me, lowering his voice. 'Her room smells terrible! Her body has become stiff and weak. And she's in a bad mood all the time. She must go outside, breathe fresh air, mix with society again. If not, then her mental and physical health . . .' Pascal made his hand into an aeroplane and nosedived it towards the ground. 'Please will you talk to her, Clementine? Make her see reason?'

But I was just a kid! Why would she listen to me?

'I'll try, but—'

'She's *very* constipated – *zut alors!* She needs the exercise to make her do a poo-poo!'

I put on my most serious expression in an effort to control the giggles that were rising in my rib cage. To my surprise, a little giggle escaped from Pascal's lips first. He smacked his wrist and covered his mouth.

'It's not funny. It's most serious. Go on, go!' He nudged me up the stairs and disappeared into the kitchen.

I knocked on Lyn's bedroom door.

'Unless your name is Clementine, go away!' came the reply.

I opened the door and went in.

Viv immediately started squawking and hopping about on his perch.

'Put this bird out of his misery,' said Lyn. 'He's bored as bed knobs.'

'STAND AND DELIVER!' I called, patting my shoulder. Viv flew over to me, landed on my arm and hopped up on to my shoulder, butting me gently with his beak. '*Bing bong!*'

'So, Clementine, have you got another poem for me?'

I nodded. 'It's not a funny one, though,' I said.

'I'm intrigued.' She held out the marker. 'Off you go, then.'

'But,' I took the marker from her, 'as it's a bit different from my other poems maybe you should—'

'Clementine!' Lyn sighed impatiently. 'I hope you're not going to suggest I read it *before* you write it on the wall?'

Well, yes I was, actually. I shook my head.

'You should know me well enough by now to know that I'm a risk-taker.'

'What about *raclette*?' I asked. 'You didn't risk trying that. You wanted baked beans on toast instead.'

'Fair point, Clementine. I'm slightly less adventurous when it comes to food. That's because I have a dodgy gut, a condition I brought upon myself back when I didn't look after my health properly. I'm actually having the opposite problem right now, but we won't go into that!'

'Do you think you're looking after your health properly now?' I asked.

'Absolutely!' said Lyn.

'Because Pascal thinks you need to get outside and move around more,' I said.

'Pascal's such a worry-wort. He's a sixty-five-year-old in the body of a twenty-seven-year-old, whereas I'm a twenty-seven-year-old in the body of a sixty-four . . . no wait . . . I've forgotten how old I am. Perhaps you'd be so kind as to google me and let me know my age. Not now, obviously – come on, let's see this poem!'

She nodded to the marker pen in my hand.

I opened up my book and approached the wall.

'STOP!' shouted Lyn, making me jump. She pointed to a paper bag on the floor next to the Union Jack chair. 'Nearly forgot. Open that bag.'

I went over to the bag and peered inside. It contained a can of orange spray paint. I lifted it out. I'd never held a can of spray paint before. It felt like I was holding a lightsaber.

'You won't be able to write the poem with that, but thought you could warm up first by adding a splash of colour. I do like orange, don't you? Give it a good shake.'

I shook the can and sprayed it against the wall. It made a satisfying hiss as I created a giant orange dribbly splodge.

'Perhaps we'd better put Viv out of harm's way. Don't want him getting high on the fumes,' she said.

I did as she said and nudged Viv back on to his perch.

'Better have a little practice first. Here, spray it on this wall, above my bed. Draw something. Anything!'

I knew better than to think about it too long. I gave the can a good shake and sprayed it in a large circle above Lyn's bedhead. Then I added two eyes and a wibbly-wobbly mouth.

Lyn twisted round to look. 'Give it some spikes.'

I added some spiky hair.

'Now spray some here.' She pointed to her shiny black duvet cover.

I pointed the can at the empty side of her bed and

pressed the nozzle. A large orange splodge appeared and dribbled over the edge.

Lyn whooped. 'Right, now you can write your poem with the marker and use the spray paint to give it a frame.'

I was about to do as I was told but a thought popped into my head.

'First, you need to get out of bed and stretch your legs,' I said.

'Beg pardon?' said Lyn.

'You need to start doing some exercise – or else you'll get ill again. Just put your skates on, and skate around your bed and back. Then I'll begin.'

Lyn stared at me. I couldn't tell whether my cheekiness had made her blood boil or whether she was secretly impressed.

'Please?' I begged.

Slowly she folded back the duvet, shifted herself towards the edge of the bed and slipped her feet into her roller skates.

'I'm only doing this because I want to see your poem,' she grumbled, lifting the rope from the floor.

I watched as she shuffled clumsily around the edge of her bed to the far side and back again.

'There!' She kicked off the skates and climbed back in. 'Happy?'

'Maybe next time you could roller skate down the street and back?' I suggested.

Lyn threw back her head and laughed. 'I'd expect a full anthology for that.'

'A full what-ology?'

'Never mind. Look it up when you get home.'

I returned to the poem wall, held open my book and copied out my words with the marker pen in the space between my 'Autumn' poem and Pascal's flamingo. Once again, it was a bit wonky, but I knew Lyn wouldn't be bothered about that. I then picked up the spray paint and sprayed a curly-wurly orange frame around it.

'All finished?' she asked, shielding her eyes. 'Can I look now?'

'Yep.' I moved out the way so she could read.

'Oh, what a magnificent frame!' She put her glasses on and cleared her throat.

'My Kingdom
by Clementine Florentine ...

My home is my kingdom
I roam in my knickers
Slide in my socks
Eat with my fingers
Spill milk on the floor
Become a mermaid in the bath
Sing loudly with my hairbrush
Dance on the sofa
Slide down the banister
Cry when I'm sad
Shout when I'm angry
Cheer when I'm happy
I answer only to the king
Who is a pretty good king
But the king wants a queen
And we all know what happens
when the king finds a queen
Things are never the same again.'

Lyn removed her glasses and looked at me thoughtfully.

'Gosh, Clementine, I'm in awe. That's a simply stupendous poem! I can just picture you prancing around your home in your under-crackers, free to be who you are and then – it turns into a fairy tale . . . a fairy tale that sounds like it doesn't have a happy ending.' She glanced at the wall. 'I take it your dad is the king?'

I nodded.

'And is he looking for a queen?'

'He's already found one. He says it's 'early days' and they're 'just friends', at the moment,' I made little quote marks in the air like my dad did, 'but she'll be his girlfriend soon – unless . . .'

'Unless what?'

'Unless he's so freaked out by what he saw on her Facebook page that he decides to break up with her.'

'Why? What did he see on her Facebook page?' Lyn pulled herself upright.

'On her 'About' page it says she's married to Raymond Norris – that's my dad's name.'

Lyn frowned. 'Why on earth would she say that if it isn't true? It doesn't make sense. Surely there's no faster way to destroy a blossoming romance?'

I shrugged and shifted my weight awkwardly from one foot to the other.

Lyn narrowed her eyes. 'Does this woman seem a bit cuckoo?'

'She has a laugh like a horse and acts really, really fake.'

'Aaah ... *Neigh* ...' Lyn smiled, her eyes rolling towards the first word I wrote on her wall. 'So, she's not cuckoo – just not your cup of tea.'

'It was her son who called my poem rubbish – the one who won the poetry competition. Callum.'

Lyn's eyebrows rose by a couple of centimetres. 'Aha! The plot thickens!'

I went and stood by Viv and tickled him under his chin.

'So, you're not keen on your dad's choice of girlfriend?' asked Lyn.

I shook my head.

'But your dad seems keen on her?'

'Kind of. But I know if they split up, he'd get over it.' I was pretty sure of that. Dad always said he was at his happiest sitting on the sofa between Lottie and me, eating popcorn and watching *Britain's Got Talent*.

'And what about the boy, Callum?' said Lyn. 'How does he feel about your parents' friendship?'

'He wants his parents to get back together. We hate each other, but we agree on one thing: my dad and his mum aren't a good match.'

Lyn raised an eyebrow. 'I see.'

I put the spray paint back in the bag and sat down in the Union Jack chair.

'I used to 'act fake', you know,' said Lyn.

'How do you mean?' I'd never heard anyone admit to being fake before. It just wasn't something you fessed up to.

'Back in my punk days. Pretended to be a loud-mouthed cockney hard nut like Johnny Rotten – but that wasn't really me. I was definitely a lot softer round the edges than I let on. I wanted to shock and impress people. Wanted to be accepted. It's taken me a long time to learn to just be myself.'

I sort of got what she meant, but not totally.

'So, I'm wondering if maybe Callum's mum seems fake to you because she's trying a bit too hard to make you like her?' said Lyn. 'As for her Facebook page, it could've been hacked by someone with an ulterior motive?'

I shrugged and looked away.

'The main question is . . . does she make your dad happy?'

I thought about Dad humming cheerfully while he spring cleaned the house. How differently he dressed and did his hair when she was around. How he grinned dreamily at her selfie. How they were always laughing their heads off together. I didn't want to answer Lyn's question, so I shrugged again. Luckily, she changed the subject.

'So how about this spoken word competition, then? Have you decided to take the plunge?'

'Don't know.'

'Come on, Clementine!' Lyn clenched her fists. 'You're a great poet and I know you can do this.'

I could feel my heart glowing brighter from Lyn's words of praise. Even though my dad often told me I was a great poet, hearing it from someone else made it seem more convincing – especially from someone who knew about writing songs and poems. Her opinion mattered to me.

'Be brave and take the risk!' urged Lyn.

'I will if you will,' I said, standing up.

'I will if you will what?'

'Take a risk. I'll enter the spoken word competition if you'll come and watch me perform.'

Lyn looked startled.

'You want me to get out of bed, get dressed, leave the house and come to your school? You want me to break my bed-in?'

'Yes,' I said. 'It'd be good for you to get out, get some fresh air, get moving and have some fun!'

Lyn sank back into her pillows and pulled her duvet up to her chin.

'I'm sorry, Clementine, but no, that won't be possible.'

CHAPTER 18

MONDAY

AS WE WALKED TO SCHOOL THE NEXT MORNING, ROM WAS BEING VERY QUIET. SULKY, EVEN.

'What's up?' I asked her.

'Well, shortly after we texted each other yesterday, I texted you again and I never got a reply, which is what you'd call RUDE.'

Dagnammit! I must've missed it among all those messages from Callum.

'And then there's the fact you were supposed to come to my house for a sleepover but got grounded. I even got my mum to buy chocolate popcorn!'

Chocolate popcorn? *Double dagnammit!*

'I'm sorry about that but you should be backing me up, not making me feel bad!' I protested.

'I'm not trying to make you feel bad, but maybe this plan to get rid of Callum's mum isn't worth it?'

'Seriously, Rom, I was gutted to miss our sleepover – but I guess it was a necessary sacrifice in order to avoid having Neigh-Neigh for a step-mum and Callum for a step-brother. Don't you get that?'

'I get that you don't want it right now, but maybe if you give them both a chance? You're so obsessed with Operation Bad Romance, it's like you've become a different person. Maybe Callum's not so bad? Maybe Neigh-Neigh's not so bad?'

Clearly Rom had lost her mind and her memory. We were talking about the boy who rubbished my poem when he didn't even know me and has never once said anything nice to me – even when he's been a guest in my house! How could she not see the horrible situation I was in?

'I thought you were supposed to be my friend!' I snapped and stormed ahead.

'I thought you were supposed to be mine!' she called after me.

When the bell rang for lunch, I kept my back to Rom (as I'd done all morning) and approached Mr C as the rest of the class filed out of the classroom.

'Clementine?' He smiled at me. 'What can I do for you?'

All morning I'd felt a poem brewing in the pit of my stomach. A poem about what happens when the queen moves into the king's palace and starts to take over. It would be a very tricky poem to write, as my dad would be there watching me perform it and I needed the words to reach his heart and make him see reason. It would be my most challenging poem yet.

'Is it too late for me to sign up for the spoken word competition?' I asked.

Mr C beamed at me. 'Of course it's not too late! I'm thrilled you want to enter. Your act mustn't be more than five minutes long, and I advise you to rehearse as much as you can as the show's just around the corner. Oh – and you can wear your own clothes. Sound OK?'

'Yes,' I nodded. 'Sounds OK.'

'Sweet.' He fist-bumped me. 'So pleased you're joining us, Clementine.'

When I collected my tray of food in the canteen, I realised that there was nowhere to sit. Rom was sitting on a table with all my other classmates and the only free seats I could see were on a table where Callum was sitting – alone. I trudged over reluctantly and plonked myself down as far away from him as I possibly could.

'Tangerine,' he said, laying down his fork and pushing his leftover pasta spirals to one side.

'Gollum,' I replied. (Gollum! How had I not thought of it sooner?) I continued to ignore him while cutting up my sausages and admiring the smooth dome of mashed potato that would soon be in my stomach.

'Operation Bad Romance is over,' he said. 'I'm out.'

Um, excuse me? I looked at him like he was mad. 'But we're so *close*!' I said. 'I'm pretty sure my dad is on the verge of splitting up with your mum.'

'It doesn't matter any more,' he said. 'I'm done.'

'Why?'

'Why d'you think, Sherlock?' He glowered at me.

I shrugged.

'You're SO dense,' he sighed. 'Did you seriously think

my mum wouldn't realise I'd hacked her account? And that I wouldn't get into trouble?'

'*Of course* you were going to get into trouble,' I said matter-of-factly, 'but those are the sacrifices we have to make if we want our cause to succeed.'

I was beginning to sound a lot more like a freedom fighter than Lottie ever would.

Callum leant back in his seat and glared at me. 'My mum is really, *really* upset. I've been grounded from now until the middle of next century. And even though I want her to get back with my dad, all our plan is doing is making things worse.'

'It can't possibly make things worse,' I argued.

'Maybe not for you!' Callum blurted. 'Hacking into her account was a step too far. I wish I hadn't done it. She might never forgive me.'

I wish I could say I felt sorry for Callum, but I didn't. He deserved every bad thing that happened to him.

'You haven't told your mum about Operation Bad Romance, have you?' I asked.

'No, fungus-features, I haven't. But I'll tell you this much – I wish I'd never listened to you.'

'Well no one forced you to,' I said. 'Although it must be

hard to think for yourself when you've got the micro-brains of a goldfish.'

'And you'd know all about goldfish, after stuffing a dead one in my mum's bag – you PSYCHO!' He picked up a pasta spiral and threw it at me. It hit me in the chest and rolled into my lap. I flicked it on to the floor.

'You're SUCH a moron!' I growled. I searched my plate for something I could fire back at him, but I didn't want to waste my bangers and mash. I kicked myself for not getting peas.

Another pasta spiral hit me in the face. Followed by another.

'Stop it, you hairy butt-wipe!' I shouted. But he carried on. Enough was enough. I picked up my beloved ball of mashed potato (such a tragic waste) and lobbed it at him. It hit him right between the eyes – an epic shot if I do say so myself.

Just then, Mrs Simpkins stormed towards us, her pencil-thin eyebrows pressed together in the shape of a V.

'WHAT IN THE NAME OF IDIOCY DO YOU THINK YOU'RE DOING?' she screeched.

My heart started pounding. My body started shaking. This was it – I was finally going to be Simpkinned. Callum's eyes were wide, his mouth gaping, the cockiness drained away. He hadn't been in this school long enough to

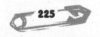

understand that he was about to suffer a far worse trauma than anything he'd ever experienced before.

'Get up!' she barked.

We stood up. She snatched my dinner tray from the table and parked it on a nearby trolley.

'Both of you follow me.' She beckoned with a long, blood-red claw.

As we pivoted round to follow her, I stopped in my tracks. There was Lottie, her mouth wide open, standing behind me with a group of Year Fours, staring at me like I was a monster.

Uh-oh. How much had she heard? Definitely the dead fish bit.

'MOVE IT!' shrieked Mrs Simpkins.

Two minutes later we were standing in Mrs Barraclough's office, staring at her super-straight fringe while she studied her computer screen, pretending to ignore us. On her desk was a packet of chewing gum (seriously?) and a framed photograph of her wife. I noticed Mrs Barraclough was wearing a T-shirt with something written on it but as her blazer was covering some of the letters, I could only make out the middle of each word: *ucati r Mart*. Hmm . . . There was definitely something familiar about those letters.

Finally she looked up, stared right at me and then at Callum.

'Why were you throwing food at each other?' She fixed me with a hard stare.

'He started it,' I said.

Mrs Barraclough gave a loud, fake, yodely yawn that made us both flinch. 'Those three little words always make me feel so sleepy for some reason.' She turned to Callum. 'Did you start it?'

'Yes,' he said. 'I threw my pasta at her.'

Callum was *owning it?* I was sort of impressed – but bewildered too. *You're supposed to blame it on the other person, dummy.*

'I would've poured my water over her head, too, but Mrs Simpkins came over before I had the chance,' he added.

Seriously? Didn't he know the meaning of 'quit while you're ahead'? Callum needed to get a grip before he got himself suspended.

Oh. I seeee.

Is that what he was trying to do? Get himself suspended?

'I sort of wound him up,' I said. 'I made him angry.'

Mrs Barraclough frowned at me. 'Do go on, Clementine. Why would you do that?'

If we told her about our parents going out with each

other, we could end up telling her all about Operation Bad Romance and no good could possibly come of that.

'I just don't like him,' I said.

'And I don't like her either,' said Callum.

Mrs Barraclough swished her hair over her shoulders and folded her arms.

'It's quite OK not to like each other. We can't like everybody – I perfectly understand that. But you *do* have to learn to be civil towards people you don't like – particularly in school where you're faced with each other every day. Today you've behaved like a couple of spoilt toddlers. I'll be phoning your parents to explain to them why you'll both be having lunchtime detentions for the rest of the week. And if there's any more of this infantile behaviour, you'll both be suspended. Is that clear?'

'Yes, Mrs Barraclough,' we replied.

'Before I dismiss you both,' she continued, 'I'd like to ask Callum: how're you getting on? I do appreciate that moving homes and schools can be very stressful. Hopefully you're starting to settle in?'

Callum's lip started to quiver. He bit down on it, but a tear broke free from his eye and rolled down his cheek.

'Clementine, go and finish your lunch. Callum, perhaps

we'd better have a chat . . .'

I left her office in silence and returned to the almost-empty canteen, where Mrs Simpkins was waiting with my cold sausages and gravy. I didn't have the courage to ask if there was any mash going spare.

As I sat there, eating on my own, I thought about Callum and that runaway tear. He'd probably hate me more than ever now that I'd actually seen him cry. He'd know I could tell everyone if I wanted and get him back for how he made me feel when he said my poem was rubbish. But getting revenge didn't seem so appealing any more. He wasn't quite as tough as he made himself out to be. He was just a boy missing his dad, his friends, his old life. If I was finding our parents' relationship hard to adjust to, he was finding it way harder. We were in the same boat – so was there any point in being at war?

Meanwhile, I had more pressing worries to deal with. Dad would go ballistic when I got home. I'd barely got back in his good books after being rude to Neigh-Neigh, and now he was going to get a phone call from Mrs Barraclough about my behaviour at school, and then Lottie would seal my death warrant by spilling the beans on Operation Bad Romance and my fishy behaviour.

This time, the punishment would be harsh.

CHAPTER 19

A FEW HOURS LATER...

I WALKED HOME ALONE. ROM WAS ONLY TWENTY PACES AHEAD OF ME, BUT I WASN'T READY TO MAKE FRIENDS AGAIN YET — ESPECIALLY AFTER SHE'D BEEN SO UNFAIR. I LOOKED AT THE FRIENDSHIP BRACELET SHE'D BROUGHT ME BACK FROM ITALY AND FIXED TO MY WRIST. MY HEAD WAS A MESS. I FELT ALL BOBCOMDISULATED. OR WAS IT DISBOBCOMBULATED?

If Neigh-Neigh was really upset, and angry at Callum for hacking her Facebook account, was that a good thing or a bad thing? Was she upset because Callum had invaded her

privacy or because the words 'married to Raymond Norris' had freaked my dad out and made her look like a crazy person? I really wanted to ask my dad what he thought of her Facebook page, but I wasn't supposed to know about it. And anyway, he'd have had that phone call from Mrs Barraclough by now, so I was pretty much walking towards the end of my life as a free person.

Rom turned off towards her house without a backwards glance. I slowed my pace down. No point rushing. Then again, I might as well get it over and done with. I was going to get a blasting – there was no escaping it. I guessed Dad would confiscate my phone, plus issue a complete screen ban and/or sugar ban for at least a week. The sugar ban was what worried me most because past warnings had taught me that it included everything from Crunchy Nut Cornflakes to vanilla yoghurt, and I wasn't sure I'd survive. And there was no chance of Lottie defending me, now that she knew what I'd done to Mr Miyagi. I wouldn't just be getting grief from Dad, I'd be getting it from her, too – most likely in a hail of arrows or a bedroom full of booby traps. Then I remembered she had taekwondo club today. After Dad was done with me, I'd hopefully still have time to stockpile food and barricade myself in my room.

When I got home, I opened the front door with my key and paused on the doorstep. This was it. *Bye-bye, Clementine Florentine. It's been nice knowing you. You were a strong woman with a passionate heart. You had the makings of a great poet, but sadly you didn't live long enough for the world to recognise your great talent.*

I pushed open the front door and stepped inside. Voices were coming from Dad's study, and one of those voices was Neigh-Neigh's. I closed the door gently, tiptoed along the hallway and, keeping out of sight, peered through the crack between the door's hinges.

Dad was sitting at his computer with his back to me. I looked around for Neigh-Neigh before noticing she was right in front of him – on his computer screen. Her face looked different. I wasn't sure why. Then I realised it was because she wasn't her usual super-smiley self and had trails of smudged mascara beneath her eyes.

'I'm sorry, Ray. It's too little, too late,' she said.

'Look, I'm sorry if my reaction was a bit abrupt,' said Dad. 'I should've guessed there was a simple explanation. I just panicked and thought people would talk and it would get back to my kids and might upset them. Clementine, in particular, is finding this a bit hard to get her head around.'

'So is Callum.'

'Did you get a call from school today?' asked Dad.

'Yes,' sighed Neigh-Neigh. 'So that's another reason we should probably call it a day. I mean, it's not worth coaching them through this if we can't even communicate with each other properly. When you ignored my calls, it made me feel rejected and vulnerable. It *hurt*. I don't need those feelings in my life right now, Ray. I've been through enough of that already.'

'I'm really sorry. I've been an idiot. I should've answered your call.' Dad ran his fingers through his hair. 'This is all new territory for me. It's been a long time since I dated someone and I'm completely out of practice. Can't we put this behind us and continue where we left off?'

Neigh-Neigh shook her head. 'I'm sorry. Look, I've got to go now but this just isn't working. Hopefully we can still be friends. I'll see you around.'

She vanished from the screen. Dad lowered his head into his hands and sat very still.

I was about to pretend I'd just walked in the front door when I heard a soft whimpering sound – a bit like the sound Eddie made when he was on the verge of exploding with kibble.

Was Dad crying?

The whimpering sound grew louder. I shrank away from the study door. I'd never seen or heard my dad cry before. Ever.

I didn't even know he *could* cry.

What should I do?

After a minute or two I knocked on the door (I never knock) and waited for him to answer.

'Come in,' he said, blowing his nose. 'Didn't know you were back, Clem.'

I went in, dumped my bag on the ground and threw my arms around him. Dad squeezed me tight and cried a bit more.

'Dad, why are you crying?' I asked, kneeling on the floor by his chair.

I mean, I knew he'd just broken up with Neigh-Neigh, but surely it wasn't *that* big a deal?

My heart caught in my throat as a frightening thought occurred to me. 'Are you dying?' My eyes welled up.

'No, I'm not dying.' He mopped his eyes with a tissue. 'Boys *do* cry, you know, Clem. Even grown-up ones. I've not handled a situation very well. I hurt Mel's feelings and now she doesn't want to see me any more.'

'But you can find another girlfriend!' I said cheerfully. *Not one who neighs or has an annoying son. And not now. In a few years' time. Maybe.*

'Finding a partner is harder than you think,' said Dad. 'A partner that you really get on with; have a laugh with. Mel's the first person who I've felt that kind of connection with since me and your mum split up – and I've blown it.' Dad shook his head and closed his eyes. 'What an utter idiot.'

'Who's an utter idiot? Callum?'

'No – ME!' Dad gave a sad laugh. '*I'm* the idiot. All she wanted to do was talk yesterday, but I filtered her calls.'

'Why didn't you want to talk to her?'

'I don't know.' Dad looked at me and shrugged. 'I really don't know. I felt a bit angry about her Facebook status, even though it wasn't her fault. I think the words *'married to Raymond Norris'* stirred up a lot of mixed feelings for me. Why am I telling you this? You're too young to understand.'

'No, I'm not!' I protested. 'You can talk to me. Just don't use too many long words like disbobulated.'

Dad smiled. 'OK. I miss what I had with your mum. I want to have that closeness with someone again. Mel and I – we just clicked. We have the same sense of humour. She's warm and funny, kind and clever. I really enjoy – *enjoyed* –

her company. I love you and Lottie with all my heart, but I don't want to be single forever. I want to share my life with someone.'

It had never occurred to me that Dad needed anyone else in his life, because he had me and Lottie.

'Sometimes it's the little things,' he said. 'Me and your mum always used to have a late-night bowl of Shreddies while watching the news headlines. We called it the Ten O'clock Shredlines. I'm not saying I want to get back with Mum – but I need to move on and find someone I can connect with. I *need* that, Clem.'

I looked down at the floor. I'd got what I wanted – Neigh-Neigh was history. But instead of feeling like jumping for joy, I had this horrible feeling I'd made a huge mistake. My dad was miserable. I remembered Lyn's question: 'Does she make him happy?' The answer, whether I wanted to admit it or not, was 'yes'. And I *wanted* him to be happy. I couldn't bear to see him like this.

A niggly feeling was growing inside me, spreading up from my body into my head: *guilt*.

I'd created this whole situation. Sure, I'd got Callum to help with my cunning plan, but it had basically been my idea. I'd been so wrapped up in keeping things the way they were, I hadn't seen that my dad was lonely – that he needed someone his own age to share things with.

And now I'd gone and ruined it for him.

'Just talk to her again, Dad,' I said.

Dad frowned. 'I'm surprised to hear you say that. After all, you're not exactly Mel's number one fan, are you?'

'Maybe she's not that bad,' I said.

Dad reached across his desk and picked up a familiar-looking book.

My poem book! *NOOO!*

'After I received that phone call from Mrs Barraclough earlier, I decided to do something I'd never normally do, and read your poem book. I thought it would help me to understand what was going on in your head.'

I flopped on to my butt, the blood draining from my limbs.

He opened the book.

> 'I hate her with all of my heart
> She's tearing my family apart
> How dare she pretend to like me!
> Does she do it just to spite me?
> She laughs like a cartoon horse

Her cheeriness sounds really forced
If I could push her off Brighton pier
Life could go back to normal round here
I hate her with all of my heart
She smells like a big eggy fart.'

He snapped the book shut. 'I think that says it all really.'

'But I crossed that one out. It's got lines through it.'

'I've read them all, Clementine – including the 'My Kingdom' one. You felt threatened by Mel, and I understand that. Well, you don't need to worry any more because the threat is over – for the time being, anyway. If I'm lucky enough to meet someone as nice as her again, I won't make the same mistakes twice – not just the mistake of avoiding Mel's calls, but the mistakes I made in leaving it to the last minute to let you and Lottie know about stuff.' Dad glanced at his computer and got up. 'Talking of Lottie, I need to pick her up from taekwondo.'

'About Lottie . . .'

'What about Lottie?'

'She may have found out that Mr Miyagi . . . ended up in Mel's bag.'

Dad paused by the door. 'You put him in Mel's bag?

240

Hence the overpowering stench of fish?'

'I'm really sorry. It was a stupid thing to do – I was angry because you'd invited them to join us without warning me first.'

'I can understand your anger,' he said, 'but not your spitefulness.'

He dropped my poem book into my lap and went to fetch his jacket. I sat there, glued to the carpet, my poem book staring up at me.

What had I gone and done? My dad was the saddest I'd ever seen him – and it was all because of me. I was a bad, bad person. And, as if that wasn't enough, my sister now hated me, my best friend wasn't talking to me and I was currently one of the naughtiest people in my class.

How in the name of Snape's cape had I managed to dig myself into such a deep hole?

And more importantly, how in the name of Dumbledore's beard could I dig myself back out again?

CHAPTER 20

THREE MINUTES LATER . . .

WHILE DAD WAS PICKING UP LOTTIE FROM TAEKWONDO, I RUSHED ROUND TO LYN'S AND RANG THE DOORBELL. I NEEDED TO TALK TO SOMEONE. I COULDN'T PHONE MUM BECAUSE SHE WAS STILL IN HONG KONG AND IT WAS PROBABLY THE MIDDLE OF THE NIGHT THERE. BESIDES, I WASN'T EVEN SURE IF DAD HAD TOLD HER ABOUT NEIGH-NEIGH YET. I WAS HOPING LYN MIGHT BE ABLE TO TELL ME HOW TO DIG MYSELF OUT OF THE HOLE I'D DUG MYSELF INTO.

Pascal came to the door wearing a flamingo-patterned

shirt and skinny yellow jeans. I couldn't help thinking that he and Ingrid would be perfect for each other, but I banished the thought from my mind. It was probably best I stayed out of other people's love lives for the time being.

'I can't stay long,' I told him, as I tried to catch my breath. 'Is Lyn upstairs?'

'Ah, non,' he sighed. 'She went bungee jumping today – in the costume of Wonder Woman.'

'*What?*'

Pascal laughed. 'I made a joke, silly! Of course she's upstairs. Where else? Please, go up and continue the good work. Whatever you said to her last time, she must've listened because she made me order dumb-bells from the internet. Just little ones, but it is a good start. Exercise in bed is better than no exercise at all, *n'est-ce pas*?'

I ran upstairs and knocked on Lyn's door. There was no answer, so I eased the door open and stepped inside. Lyn wasn't in her bed. Viv squawked at me from his perch and started bobbing up and down – a sign that he was pleased to see me. Humming was coming from inside her en suite bathroom, so I made my way over to Viv and invited him to sit on my shoulder.

'Oh, for crying out loud, just bloody get on with it, will

243

you?!' shouted Lyn, from the other side of her bathroom door.

'Um, well, I was waiting for you to come out first,' I said, taken aback by her grumpy tone.

'Clementine?'

'Yes.'

'Oh. I was talking to myself. Make yourself comfortable. I'll be out in a minute.'

Viv and I exchanged looks.

'Hallelujah! SUCCESS!' cheered Lyn. The loo flushed, the bathroom tap went on and off and she shuffled out on her roller skates, clutching her rope and rubbing her lower back. 'Clementine, what can I do for you?' she smiled.

'I haven't got long – my dad doesn't know I'm here.'

'You look flustered. What's wrong?'

'My dad found my poem book and read all my poems about Neigh-Neigh – including that one.' I pointed to the wall.

Lyn followed the direction of my finger. '*Neigh-Neigh? Is that what you call your dad's girlfriend?*'

'Ex-girlfriend.'

'I see . . . You'd better bring me up to date.'

As Lyn got into bed, I quickly told her everything, from

Operation Bad Romance to my fight with Callum in the school canteen, to falling out with Rom and seeing Dad cry.

'I think I've made a terrible mistake,' I said. 'And if Dad thinks my poems are mean, what would he think of all my scheming and plotting? He'd never forgive me. I'm a terrible person!' I started to cry. 'Even my best friend thinks I'm a bad person.'

Lyn patted the side of her bed. 'Come and sit over here.'

I sat by her feet and stroked Viv's feathers while he nuzzled my cheek. It was as if Viv was trying to wipe away my tears.

'Firstly, you're not a terrible person – you're human,' said Lyn. 'And humans make mistakes. We *all* behave badly from time to time. Secondly, *of course* your dad will forgive you. He may be a bit cross with you for a while, but when I met him, he didn't strike me as the type of bloke to bear a grudge against his own child just because she found it hard to adapt to him having a girlfriend. And fourthly—'

'Thirdly,' I corrected her.

'And thirdly, you could always try to put things right and redeem yourself.'

'How?' I asked. The idea of fessing up gave me a very windy tummy ache.

'Well, firstly, with regards to your best friend, the word 'sorry' goes a long way. And fourthly—'

'Secondly.'

'And secondly, with regards to everything else . . . is Callum entering the spoken word competition?'

'Yes.'

'Well, why don't you propose to him that you join forces? Do a double act – a plea to your parents to give things another go!'

NO WAY, JOSÉ.

That was a ridiculous idea. Callum would laugh me out of the classroom, out of the school gates and all the way home.

'There's no way he'd agree to it. He's *pleased* it's over between them. All he wants is for his parents to get back together, remember?'

'Clementine, if Callum has moved house, moved school and moved city, I'd imagine things are pretty final between his parents – and deep down he knows that. His poem certainly gave the impression there was no going back. Meanwhile, you said yourself he didn't want to pursue Operation Bad Romance any more, so why don't you just ask him? If you're already feeling this terrible, what have you got to lose?'

She had a point. Nothing could make me feel any worse than I already did.

'Even if he doesn't mind our parents seeing each other any more, he wouldn't want to do a poem with *me*. He already made it quite clear what he thinks of my poetry.'

'You said his mum was angry with him for tampering with her Facebook page?'

I nodded.

'And it sounds like his mum's pretty disappointed with how things have turned out with your dad?'

I nodded again.

'Well, maybe he could do with an opportunity to redeem himself, too?'

Again, she had a point.

'What if he says no? Then what?' I asked.

'Then you'll have to go it alone. Use the spoken word competition as an opportunity to make your dad proud of you,' she beamed.

I stared at the wall ahead of me. I certainly needed to do something to make Dad proud of me. And the poem I'd been planning on writing was suddenly no longer necessary. Perhaps now I needed to write a poem that could turn everything around?

'If Callum won't team up with me, I'm not sure I can do it alone,' I said, hoping Lyn might take the hint and offer to come along and support me.

She sighed. 'Yes, you can, Clementine. You're stronger than you realise.'

'So are you.'

I was starting to find Lyn's bed-in annoying. I couldn't see the point of it – it's not like you can avoid things forever, so you might as well get it over and done with. And, more than anything, I really wanted her to be there in the audience, cheering me on. I'd never performed my own writing out loud before and the thought of it made me feel almost dizzy with nerves. If she were there, I'd feel better because I knew she believed in me so it wouldn't matter what anyone else thought.

'You could come to the show if you wanted,' I mumbled.

She gave me a sorrowful look. 'I'll be supporting you all the way, *I promise* – just without leaving my bed. You can come and rehearse here, if you like. But me, leave this room?' She shook her head. 'The thought of going outside just fills me with dread to be honest.'

'But I thought your bed-in was only for a year? You can't avoid going outside for ever – that's crazy!'

'Punk is dead!' chirped Viv.

I stood up and set Viv back on his perch.

'I've got to go,' I said, frustration surging inside me. 'Thanks for the advice.'

Lyn reached for her novel. 'Keep me posted.'

As I opened her bedroom door, I turned around. My heart was hammering and my mouth had gone dry – a sign I had something important to say but didn't have the courage to say it. Was there any point in saying what I thought? It's not like it would make any difference.

Then again, what did I have to lose?

'I guess Viv is right,' I croaked. 'Punk *is* dead.'

CHAPTER 21

TUESDAY

THE FOLLOWING MORNING, WHILE EATING CRACKERS AND CHEESE FOR BREAKFAST, I GOT A TEXT FROM ROM SAYING SHE WAS GETTING A LIFT TO SCHOOL WITH HER MUM. IT WASN'T AN INVITATION FOR ME TO JOIN HER — BUT A WARNING I'D BE ON MY OWN. MY HEART SANK A LITTLE. I DIDN'T THINK OUR FALL OUT WOULD LAST LONGER THAN A FEW HOURS.

I had a lot of work to do: I needed to gain my best friend's respect again, earn Lottie's forgiveness, get properly, totally back into Mr C's good books, write an amazing poem

and make Dad proud of me again.

'Um, Rom isn't walking with me this morning,' I told Dad as he munched his toast.

'You can walk with us, then,' said Dad.

'I'm not walking with *her*.' Lottie shot me a dirty look. 'You treated Mr Miyagi like a dog biscuit and you made Dad and Mel split up.'

'I know I haven't been a very nice person lately,' I said, 'but I'm going to make up for it, I promise.'

'You can start by tidying my room after school!' said Lottie.

'Fair enough,' I agreed. Lottie looked surprised. I smiled: 'You're looking at the *new me*.'

'Would the *new you* like to get a move on? It's nearly time to leave,' grumbled Dad.

When I walked into the cloakroom, Rom was hanging up her jacket. As soon as she saw me, she turned her back on me. It was time to put things right. I took a deep breath and went and tapped her on the shoulder.

'What?' she huffed.

'Rom, I'm sorry,' I began. 'I've been a rubbish friend to you recently.'

'You're right – *very* rubbish,' she said coldly. 'You've been like a crazy person.'

'I know. I've been trying to control everything because I thought if I could get things back to how they were, then we'd all be much happier – or at least, *I'd* be happier. I never imagined my meddling would make so many people miserable – most of all my dad. And how can I be happy when everyone else is miserable? I even made my *best friend* miserable. Can we be friends again?'

Rom frowned. 'I don't know. You didn't treat me very nicely. You really hurt my feelings.'

'I know. I'm so sorry. Can you forgive me? Please?'

'I know it hasn't been easy for you,' she sighed. 'But you do need to stop this crazy Operation Bad Romance.'

'That's so over,' I said. 'Although . . .' I winced at how Rom was going to take this. 'As I need to repair the damage I've done, I'm now kind of working on Operation Good Romance.'

Rom rolled her eyes. 'Seriously, Clem, just quit while you're ahead! I mean, surely you should just stay out of things from now on?'

'Just hear me out,' I said, unzipping my jacket and hanging it up on my peg. I explained what I planned to propose to Callum.

Rom weighed it up. 'OK, when you put it like that, I suppose it's worth a try.'

'So, are we friends again?' I asked.

Rom smiled. 'Yeah.'

We hugged and walked into the classroom where Luke McDonut and his friends were sitting on top of their desks and laughing. Callum was sitting in his chair looking like he'd rather be anywhere else.

'This spoken word competition is a stupid idea,' scoffed Luke, swinging a pair of headphones round in circles centimetres from Callum's head. 'I mean, who likes poetry anyway? Apart from Billy Boffin here.' His friends sniggered.

'I do,' I said, slinging my bag under my desk. 'I like poetry. *A LOT*.'

'Yeah, so do I,' said Rom.

'And so do *you*,' I grinned at Luke. 'By the sound of it.'

'Eh?' He frowned. 'What on earth are you on about, *Phlegmentine*?'

'Allow me to explain, *Puke*. You're listening to a song, right?' I pointed to his headphones and the tinny voice

echoing out of the earbuds.

He looked at me like I was stupid. 'Duh, obviously.'

'Poetry,' I said.

'*What?* Don't be insane – it's pop music!'

'Which is basically poetry set to music.'

'Songwriting *is* poetry,' Rom chimed in. Murmurs of agreement rippled around the room – even from Luke's cronies.

'Whatevs,' shrugged Luke. 'A play or talent show would've been a way better idea than a stupid spoken word competition.'

'Actually, McDonut,' said Rom, 'the spoken word competition has a bit of play and a bit of talent competition mixed in, so it's like both, but with poetry too, and so *way* more interesting.'

The classroom door banged shut and everyone quickly slid into their seats as Mr C strode into the room and frisbeed his trilby hat towards the peg on the far wall. It missed.

'Hang that up for me, would you, Luke?' he said as he dropped a pile of books on to his desk. 'Glad to hear you're all discussing the spoken word competition. I've looked through the list of acts and I'm very excited. It promises to be a versatile and highly entertaining night. In the meantime, I'm pleased to announce that the fabulous Ingrid Partridge, who you'll all remember fondly from reception year, is going to be our compère – that is to say, our host – for the evening.'

Everyone cheered – even Luke McDonut managed a smile. Everyone loved Ingrid.

'Glad you approve,' said Mr C. 'And myself, Mrs Barraclough and Ms Wallace will form the panel of judges. Just one more thing – my fellow judges and I think it would be nice if we could invite a guest to perform on the evening. I did ask a poet friend of mine but they can't make it, so if any of you know someone who's a bit of a performer, preferably someone who pens their own material, perhaps you could let me know or ask them to get in touch with the school office. Right, we'd better get on with the register.'

My heart leapt: *Lyn!*

Lyn was a performer who wrote her own material. She'd be PERFECT as a guest performer at the spoken word competition! Except, there was no way on earth she'd agree. She wasn't even willing to come and *watch*, let alone perform. Unless I could somehow persuade her . . . ?

It wasn't until our lunchtime detention that I finally got the chance to propose my new idea (or rather Lyn's idea) to Callum. While Mr C stood in the classroom doorway, chatting to Ms Wallace, I cupped my hand in front of my mouth and hissed to get Callum's attention.

'Shut up,' he hissed back. 'You've landed me in enough trouble already.'

'Just give me a chance,' I said. 'I've got an idea.'

'Are you mad? Your ideas are *bad news*. Just leave me alone.'

'But this time, it's a good idea that could maybe make good things happen,' I persisted.

'For the last time, Tangerine – SHUT UP!'

I was about to go ahead and explain what my idea was anyway when Mr C turned round.

'I'll be back in a sec,' said Ms Wallace, patting him on the shoulder and disappearing from view.

'There's not supposed to be any talking in detention!' said Mr C, walking back to his desk. 'Unless you want to extend the sentence for an extra week?' He eyeballed us

both. 'Clementine? Your mouth is open. Is there something you wanted to say?'

'Um, yes.' I swallowed. It was time to be brave. 'I wanted to tell Callum that I'm sorry for getting him in trouble. It's all my fault.'

Callum did a double take.

'You see, my dad and his mum were sort of dating and neither of us were very happy about it, so I convinced Callum that we should try to split them up.'

Mr C sat down on his desk and folded his arms. 'Okaay . . . Carry on.'

'So, we made things really awkward for them and, to cut a long story short, we succeeded in breaking them up. But the problem is, my dad is now sad and lonely and wishing he'd handled things better with N—' I stopped myself in the nick of time. 'With Mel, Callum's mum.'

Mr C looked at Callum.

'Callum? Is there anything you'd like to say?'

Callum stared hard at his desk. For a minute I wasn't sure what he was going to do – turn on me, burst into tears, or just stay frozen like that forever? Eventually, he looked up at Mr C.

'I didn't want my mum to have a new boyfriend, so when

Clementine said we should try to split them up, it seemed like a good idea. I figured I'd be doing Mum a favour cos Clementine's dad just didn't seem right for her anyway. So I did some stupid things that really hurt my mum's feelings, and now we're both really upset and she's asked me if I'd rather go and live with my dad – seeing as I've made it clear I hate it here.'

'And would you rather live with your dad?' asked Mr C.

'No,' said Callum. 'He's got back with his girlfriend and they've moved in together, so I think I'd rather stay here.'

'And is life really so bad here?' Mr C smiled.

Callum shrugged. 'Maybe not.'

'And what about Clementine's apology? Do you accept it?'

'Yeah, apology accepted,' said Callum. 'But I'm not interested in her latest idea.'

Mr C turned back to me. 'And what is your latest idea, Clementine, if you don't mind me asking?'

I blushed. 'Um, well, I've been thinking about things and . . .' *How to put this?* 'And, well, maybe Callum's mum and my dad were more right for each other than we realised . . .' I glanced nervously at Callum – he wasn't showing any signs of disagreeing with me, so I continued – 'And maybe we

didn't give them enough of a chance to get to know each other better. So, I was thinking we could maybe make it up to them and show them that we've changed by doing a joint act in the spoken word competition.'

Callum's eyes widened as if he'd just seen a gargantuan spider crawling across his desk.

'Callum?' Mr C smiled at him. 'What do you think about that?'

He'd gone into a trance again, his eyes fixed on the map above the whiteboard.

'Personally,' said Mr C, 'I think that sounds like an awesome idea.'

'I mean, they probably won't get back together,' I said. 'But maybe if we team up and write a really good poem, it might help them at least be friends again. And they might forgive us for being such doofi.'

'Doofi?' Mr C looked confused.

'One doofus, two doofi,' I explained. 'One cactus, two—'

'Got it, thanks.'

Ms Wallace reappeared in the doorway again.

'Excuse me, one second,' said Mr C. 'You carry on discussing it while I talk to Ms Wallace.'

'What do you think?' I asked Callum. 'Of course, you

probably wouldn't want to write a poem with me because I'm not as good at poetry as you are, but I've been practising a lot and—'

'You *are* good at poetry,' he mumbled.

'*What?*' Was I hearing correctly?

'I said, you are good at poetry.'

'But you said my custard creams poem was rubbish.'

'It wasn't rubbish.'

'It wasn't?' Had I misheard him at the time? No, I definitely hadn't.

'I *liked* your custard creams poem. It was clever and funny. I was being mean cos I felt jealous I hadn't thought of it myself.'

Well, curdle my cornflakes! Was I hearing this right?

Mr C waved off Ms Wallace and turned back to face us.

'So, how are negotiations coming along?' he asked. 'Callum? You don't have to say yes to Clementine's proposal. Why don't you take some time to think about it?'

'It's OK,' said Callum. 'I'm up for it. If there's a chance it'll make my mum happy again, it's worth a try.'

Mr C clapped his hands. 'Brilliant! This is going to be quite a night. Well, you'd better start working on your act right now, seeing as the show's only three days away.' He

pulled our maths sheets away from us and put them in his draw. 'Here!' He gave us some fresh paper. 'Go and sit in the far corner where it's a bit more private. I don't want to ruin a poem in progress.'

We took the paper and moved desks. As we sat down, side by side, I smiled at Callum. And for the first time ever, he smiled back at me.

CHAPTER 22

LATER THAT AFTERNOON . . .

AS SOON AS I GOT HOME FROM SCHOOL, I DECIDED TO TELL DAD THAT ME AND CALLUM HAD BECOME FRIENDS AND HAD TEAMED UP TO ENTER THE SPOKEN WORD COMPETITION.

I burst into the kitchen where Dad was boiling the kettle and fending off an arrow attack from Lottie.

'Hi!' I said.

'Time to tidy my room, *servant*!' Lottie spun round, high-kicked the air and fired an arrow at me. It narrowly missed my eye.

'LOTTIE!' shouted Dad. 'How many times have I told you

to be careful?' He marched over to her and yanked the bow out of her hands. 'The last thing I need right now is a trip to A&E.'

'Sorry!' she pleaded. 'I'll be more careful – I promise!'

'No. Enough is enough.' He grabbed the bag of arrows off her shoulder. 'This is going in the charity bag. Or the bin. Or wherever's the best place to responsibly get rid of an irresponsible present. Bloody Uncle Robert! Trust *him* to buy you something that could take an eye out. I should've confiscated this months ago.' He put it on top of the fridge where Lottie couldn't reach it.

Lottie burst into tears. 'But it's my favourite thing that I own!'

'For God's sake!' fumed Dad. 'An eye nearly gets taken out and now I've got a child in tears – all because of that brainless numbskull.'

Then Dad went and did something else I'd never seen him do before: he took a cup from the draining board and hurled it on the floor.

Lottie ran to me and buried her head in my chest.

Dad stood staring at the smashed cup. After a few deep breaths, he got out the dustpan and brush, swept it up and threw it all in the bin. Then he walked out of the room.

'It was an accident,' cried Lottie. 'I wasn't aiming for your eye on purpose, I swear!'

'I know,' I said. 'Dad's not really angry at you. If anything, he's angry at *me* for being selfish and mean to Mel.'

'Yeah, well I'm still angry with you for that, too.'

'I know, I'm sorry – I totally messed up. But don't worry, I'm already working to put things right.'

'Really? How?'

'Callum and I have become friends and we're going to do a joint act at the spoken word competition.'

'At the what competition?'

'Spoken word – it's like poetry, short stories and sketches and stuff. Both Dad and Mel will be there, so we're going to write a poem that will make them fall in love again – or at least hopefully become friends again. Or . . . I dunno . . . we just need to make up for behaving badly, I suppose.'

'So they could end up getting back together?' Lottie gripped my arm.

'It's worth a try,' I said.

'Because I *really* want to be a bridesmaid!'

'But you're a freedom fighter! Freedom fighters don't care about wearing frilly dresses and being bridesmaids.'

'THIS ONE DOES!' Lottie glared at me.

'OK, OK – I'd better go and talk to Dad.'

I found Dad sitting on his bed, staring out the window.

'Dad?' I sat down next to him. 'I'm really sorry for all the selfish things I did. I was just scared that Mel would become your favourite person and that me and Lottie wouldn't matter as much.'

'You and Lottie will always be the most important people in my life,' said Dad. 'But I can understand how the situation made you feel worried. It's new ground for all of us – and it's hard. I never was any good at the whole dating thing. Mum and I met each other at college, so we kind of missed that bit out, which means I'm pretty much a novice. Anyway, hopefully I'll be better prepared next time around.'

'Have you tried talking to Mel?'

'Yes, I tried again today, but she was pretty clear. Having gone through a painful separation with Callum's dad, it made her realise she's not ready to get into anything serious just yet.'

'Oh. Do you think she might change her mind if she knew that me and Callum are friends now?'

Dad smiled at me. 'Are you?'

'Yeah. We've put our differences to one side and we're

even going to work on a poem together for the spoken word competition.'

I expected Dad's face to light up, but it didn't. 'That's really nice, Clem.' He ruffled my hair. 'I'm very pleased to hear that. And I'm sure Mel will be pleased, too.'

'But you don't think it'll make her change her mind?'

Dad shook his head. 'It'll definitely cheer her up to know Callum's finally made a friend, though. Come on, let's go back downstairs.'

We went back down to the kitchen where Lottie was sitting hunched over the kitchen table, her head buried in her folded arms.

Dad pulled her out of her chair, picked her up and cuddled her.

'Crikey – you're heavy, Captain Foghorn.' He pulled me towards him and hugged us both at the same time. 'Team Norris, I'm very sorry for smashing a cup. It wasn't my finest moment. It's not OK to lash out and smash things. Please forgive me and learn from my many, many mistakes.'

We hugged Dad tighter.

'I love you guys so much,' he said.

'Love you, too,' we chorused.

Dad put Lottie down. 'Guess I'd better start thinking

about what to cook for dinner.'

'Pot noodles!' cheered Lottie.

Dad laughed. 'Or maybe something with some nutrients in it, Lotstable.'

While Dad looked in the fridge for nutrients, I told him what Mr C had said about wanting a guest to perform at the spoken word competition.

'Why don't you ask Lyn?' he suggested.

'I thought about that, but she won't even come to watch *me* perform, let alone perform herself,' I said. I'd already told Dad about Lyn's 'kick in the gut' so I didn't need to explain why she refused to give up her bed-in.

'If she doesn't want to come, I guess we just have to respect that, Clem-cakes,' shrugged Dad. 'You can't tell a punk rocker what to do – especially not one who's grieving for her husband and her horse.'

'But Dad, I *really* want her to come. I don't care if she doesn't perform – I just want her to be there when *I* perform. She's helped me to believe in myself. She's helped me to be a better poet. She was the one who even suggested I team up with Callum and do a joint act.'

'She's helped you that much?'

'She helped me believe in Clementine Florentine again.'

Dad gave me a sympathetic smile. 'Listen, Clem, I know Lyn seems as stubborn as a mule, but let's just be grateful she's helped you find your poetry mojo again – that's the main thing. And anyway, it goes without saying that *I'll* be there – there's no doubt about that.'

CHAPTER 23

FRIDAY

THE DAY OF THE SPOKEN WORD COMPETITION
HAD ARRIVED AND ME AND CALLUM WERE USING
THE LAST OF OUR LUNCHTIME DETENTIONS TO
TRY TO GET OUR POEM IN ORDER. WE'D BEEN
GOING ROUND IN CIRCLES, CROSSING OUT PRETTY
MUCH EVERYTHING WE'D WRITTEN SO FAR WHILE
TAKING IT IN TURNS TO CRINGE. WE'D PROMISED
NOT TO SHOW WHAT WE'D WRITTEN TO ANYONE
UNTIL THE ACTUAL NIGHT, SO WE HAD TO SOLVE
OUR PROBLEMS ON OUR OWN.

'I don't think this 'give love a chance' idea is working,'

said Callum as we sat hunched over the desks in the corner of the classroom.

'Yeah. It's way too cringe,' I agreed.

'Let's start again.'

Callum tore up the piece of paper we'd been writing on and grabbed a fresh sheet.

I'd seen Lyn a few days ago and she'd asked how our poem was coming along and whether I'd like to practise reading it to her. I told her if she wanted to hear me read it out, she'd have to come along on the night. I thought if I played hardball, she might eventually crumble, but no. Dad was right – Lyn was as stubborn as a bowl of half-eaten Weetabix left in my room for two days.

In the meantime, I wracked my brains to think of a way to make Lyn change her mind, but no ideas were coming.

'Hey!' Callum waved a hand in front of my face. 'Come on, Tangerine. Concentrate.'

'Sorry,' I said. 'I was just wondering how I could persuade my friend Lyn to come to the show.'

'Why won't she come?'

'It's a long story.'

Callum put down his pen. 'Tell me, then.'

I explained how Lyn had encouraged me to keep writing

poems and how she'd helped me to start believing in myself.

'Why didn't you believe in yourself?' asked Callum, before I even got to the whole punk-in-bed part.

'Um . . .' Should I tell him that it was mainly thanks to *him* I'd lost my confidence? I didn't want things to get all awkward again, and anyway, it was in the past. We were friends now.

'You can tell me,' he said. 'I don't always believe in myself either.'

'But you're so . . . sure of yourself!' What was he talking about?

Callum shrugged. 'Sometimes I just pretend. Coming here, to this school, I didn't feel confident at all. I didn't want to be here. I wanted to stay at my old school with my old friends. I wasn't interested in making new friends – so I suppose I didn't care what anyone thought of me to begin with. But now . . .'

'Now what?'

'Now I know that things can't go back to the way they were. My parents aren't going to get back together – they can't even speak to each other without arguing right now. I see Dad every other weekend and in the holidays. My

home's in Brighton now. This is my school. This is my life. Fighting it won't change things.'

I felt a bit sorry for him. I'd grown so used to my parents not being together any more that I'd forgotten how my life used to be. It had been such a long time since they'd last had a shouty argument, I could barely even remember it. They got on well with each other these days. Dad thought Mum's boyfriend Simon was a nice guy – even if he did think grown-up men wearing onesies was Weird 'with a capital W'. Sometimes, Mum and Simon would join us for Sunday lunch. Whatever storm we'd been through had long blown over.

'Things'll get easier, you know,' I said.

'I know,' he said. 'So why didn't you believe in yourself?'

I paused. 'When my custard creams poem didn't even come close to winning the poetry competition, and then this brainy new boy said it was rubbish, I decided I obviously wasn't as good at poetry as I liked to think I was.'

Callum flinched. 'I'm sorry. I wasn't very nice – and I didn't even mean it. I feel bad about it now.'

'It's OK. It doesn't matter any more.'

'I'm kind of surprised you believed me anyway.'

I was kind of surprised I'd believed him myself. Why had

I agreed so quickly with someone else's (not even true) opinion? How stupid was that?

We stared at the blank sheet of paper on the table in front of us.

'Hey!' I said. 'I've got an idea.'

CHAPTER 24

SHOWTIME...

THE HALL WAS FILLING UP FAST. I SAW MEL
SITTING IN THE MIDDLE LOOKING AT HER PHONE
AND TRIED TO STEER DAD AND LOTTIE TOWARDS
HER, BUT DAD PRESSED ON TOWARDS THE FRONT
WHERE LUKE MCDONUT WAS HANGING AROUND
BY THE SIDE OF THE STAGE, CLUTCHING A BOTTLE
OF COKE AND SUPPOSEDLY LOOKING AFTER THE
STAGE LIGHTING.

'Remember, I need to film it so we can send it to Mum,'
said Dad, bagging a couple of seats in the front row.

Dad and Lottie sat down while Ingrid walked over to us
wearing a bright pink jumper dress, a purple feather boa,

pink and purple polka-dot leggings and sparkly pink shoes.

'Wow,' gushed Lottie. 'Can I get a feathery scarf like that, Dad?'

Ingrid gave us a twirl. 'What d'you think of my compère outfit? Some of which was purchased with a certain 'laundered' banknote.' She winked at me. 'Thanks, babes. That took guts – literally! HA, HA!'

'You look amazing,' said Dad.

'Thank you!' said Ingrid. 'I'll catch you later – need to help Mr C gather all our performers backstage. Clem, you can follow me.'

Dad gave me a good luck punch on the arm and I followed Ingrid out of the hall into Classroom 5K, where my fellow performers were standing about clutching their poems and lines. Someone tapped me on the shoulder – Rom!

'Where's Callum?' she asked.

'I guess he's late. If you see him back in the hall, will you tell him to hurry up?'

'I would but I'm not going back in the hall because . . . Guess what?' Rom pulled a folded piece of paper out of her coat pocket and waved it around in front of me.

'What?' I said.

'I'm performing too!' she cheered.

'Seriously?' I couldn't believe it. While Rom loved it when her cakes and art got lots of attention, she didn't really like being in the spotlight herself.

'Well, back last week when you said you weren't going to enter the competition, I thought I would, just to show you that there's nothing to be scared of and your poem doesn't have to be perfect. And also, I actually really enjoyed writing my little haikus.'

'Can I see it?' I asked.

Rom snatched the piece of paper away. 'Uh-uh! It's a surprise.'

'Well, what's it about?' I pressed her.

'Let's just say it's something I've been thinking about a lot since my baby cousin Enzo was born. *So many blue gifts . . .*'

I was intrigued. 'Good luck, Romola Granola.'

'Same to you, Clementine Florentine.'

I looked around for Callum. *Where was he?*

Mr C came in and took a register of all the performing acts.

'OK, so we're just missing Callum Harvey,' he said. 'Has anyone seen him?'

'His mum's here, so he must be here, too,' I said.

Mr C and Ingrid glanced at each other, then glanced worriedly at the clock on the classroom wall.

'Right, well if you lot would like to go and take your places on the benches to the side of the stage, we'll be with you in a minute. Ms Partridge and I just need to locate Callum and then we're all set to start.'

While the others trooped back into the hall, I followed Ingrid and Mr C.

'I'll check the boys' loos, you check 6C,' said Mr C.

'Roger that,' said Ingrid, turning off down the corridor.

I followed Mr C. As we jogged through the cloakroom towards the boys' loos, something caught my eye. I stopped and blinked. A pair of shoes attached to a pair of legs were poking out of a clump of hanging coats. Callum! I ran over to where he was sitting on the floor, knees hugged to his chest, and shoved the coats to one side.

'Callum!' I gasped. 'What's the matter?'

He looked over my shoulder to make sure no one else was around.

'I can't do it.'

'Why?' I asked.

Looking nervously around him, Callum stood up and pointed to his crotch – his trousers were soaking wet.

'Oh . . .' *Poor Callum.* I squirmed with embarrassment for him. 'Gosh, I didn't realise you were so nervous,' I said.

'Don't feel bad – it could happen to anyone.'

Callum's mouth fell open. 'NOOO! It's not like that – when I came out of the loo just now, Luke was standing there with a bottle of Coke. He shook it up and aimed it at my trousers.'

Mr C saw us on his way back from the boys' loos.

'Callum!' he said, skidding to a halt. 'You OK?' His eyes fell upon Callum's wet trousers.

'It's Coke,' I explained before Mr C could get the wrong idea. 'Thanks to Luke McDonut.'

Mr C rolled his eyes. 'Is that true, Callum?'

Callum nodded.

'That boy's in BIG trouble.'

'I can't go on stage like this,' said Callum.

'Of course not,' said Mr C. 'Let me think . . . the spare clothing cupboard will be locked, and by the time I track down the key . . . Right, there's only one thing for it.'

Mr C kicked off his bright yellow trainers and started undoing his baggy jeans.

'You can wear these, Callum.' He grabbed a coat from a hook to hide behind while holding out his jeans to Callum.

Callum gawped at Mr C.

'Quick, we don't have much time.' Mr C turned his back to Callum. 'Clementine, avert your eyes, let's give Callum

some privacy here.' Mr C shooed me away. I walked to the far end of the cloakroom and faced the window, my back towards them – though I could tell Callum was still frozen.

'Callum, I know I may seem like an old fogey to you, but please don't make me feel like the most unfashionable dude on the planet by refusing to wear my jeans. Will.i.am has these jeans, you know.'

I heard Callum reluctantly unzipping his trousers. At that moment, Ingrid sprinted in and did a double take.

'Great moons of Phobos!' she squealed, shielding her eyes from Mr C's bright white underpants, which were hard to miss in the reflection of the window. 'What the peaches is going on?'

'Wardrobe malfunction,' Mr C explained over his shoulder. 'You'll need to turn up the bottoms,' he instructed Callum. 'And put the belt on the tightest notch.'

Callum shuffled about and did up the zip.

'All good? May I turn round?' asked Mr C.

'Yeah,' mumbled Callum.

'Amazing! They look better on you than they do on me,' grinned Mr C, adjusting the coat around his waist.

'What about you, though?' said Ingrid.

'I thought I had a pair of gym shorts in my desk, but I

just remembered I took them home at the end of last term, so . . .'

Mr C scratched his head. 'I've got it! My Nigerian flag – I'll take it down off the wall and wrap it round me.'

'There's no time!' yelped Ingrid. 'Here, have these.' She slid off her sparkly shoes and wriggled out of her polka dot leggings. 'Good job I wore a dress over the top!' she chuckled.

I couldn't resist turning around to see. All eyes were on Mr C as Ingrid held out her leggings.

Mr C stared at them, then inhaled sharply. 'Fine.' He took the leggings from her and slipped them on over his muscly thighs, letting go of the coat as he pulled them up to his waist and twanged the elastic.

We all started to giggle. They were so tight it was a miracle they didn't split.

Mr C slipped his trainers back on, stood up straight, shook out his shoulders and lifted his chin. 'Right, watch me own these babies,' he said proudly, strutting back out of the cloakroom. 'Come on, peeps! We need to get this party started.'

'Oh, my shimmering shoulder pads,' muttered Ingrid as we all followed him towards the hall. 'Whatever next?'

CHAPTER 25

A FEW MINUTES LATER...

A PACKED HALL ECHOED WITH GIGGLES AS WE TROOPED BACK IN AND TOOK OUR SEATS WITH THE OTHER ACTS. WHILE INGRID WAITED IN THE WINGS, MR C MADE HIS WAY TO THE STAGE, WHISPERING SOMETHING IN LUKE MCDONUT'S EAR AS HE WALKED PAST HIM. I WATCHED AS LUKE'S FACE FELL AND HIS CHEEKS FILLED WITH COLOUR.

Mr C leapt up on to the stage, did a 360-degree spin and wiggled his bottom at the audience. Then he turned round and tapped the microphone. 'I hope you like my judge's outfit.' He gestured to his polka dot-covered legs. 'It's very important that I wear something comfortable and stretchy when I'm on a judging panel, otherwise I can't give the acts the consideration they deserve.'

Everyone laughed.

'Anyway, good evening, lovely people of Brighton!' boomed Mr C.

'*Bing bong! SQUAWK!*'

'And, er, parrots?' he added, squinting towards the back of the audience.

VIV! LYN!

I craned my neck and shifted from side to side trying to catch sight of them through the sea of parents and siblings. Eventually I spotted them in the back row – Viv was perched on Lyn's shoulder and Pascal was sitting next to her. *They came!*

'Anyway, without further ado, I shall hand you over to our very special compère, the universally-adored Ms Ingrid Partridge!'

Mr C gave Ingrid a hearty clap as she skipped on to the stage, twirling the ends of her feather boa around in circles. She adjusted the mic so it was level with her cherry-red lips.

'Welcome to the Year Six spoken word competition where, tonight, ten special acts will perform in front of three very hard-to-please judges, better known as Mr C, Ms Wallace and Mrs Barraclough. Some of the acts have written their own material, while others have selected songs or familiar material that they'll put their own spin on. We had hoped to have a special guest perform for you this evening, but unfortunately we weren't able to find anyone at such short notice.'

'GORDON BENNETT!' shrieked Viv from the back row.

Ingrid laughed. 'My sentiments exactly.'

'Actually . . .' A voice came from the back row and Lyn stood up, her normally crumpled spikes brushed into a tall orange mohawk. 'I'd be happy to perform, if the invitation's still open? Clementine did ask me, but I wasn't sure if I'd be . . . *available.*'

'Great tootin' Laboutins!' exclaimed Ingrid, her face lighting up with excitement. 'Lyn? Lyn from down the road? Apparently also known as – and I can't believe I was the last person to find this out – the one and only *Lyn Ferno*?'

The adults in the audience gasped and turned to stare at the short woman with the orange hair and the parrot.

'The one and only,' said Lyn. 'Although I come with a sidekick these days.' She patted Viv. 'Oh – and don't worry, I won't do anything X-rated and I had a good burp earlier, so I'm good to go – if you'll have me, that is.'

Ingrid looked hopefully at Mrs Barraclough, whose eyes were out on stalks.

'We'd love to have you,' she stammered. 'I'm a huge fan. Thank you so much for offering.' Mrs Barraclough patted her heart and took some deep breaths. That's when I remembered the T-shirt she'd been wearing the other day and those mystery words – *Educating Mr Martian*!

'Fantastic!' boomed Ingrid. 'Cosmic cauliflowers, everyone! The evening just got even more exciting than it was already. Right, we'd better get this show on the road. Please big it up for our first act of the night, the incredibly talented Romola Narayan with her haiku-based poem, 'Kids Can Change the Rules'!'

The audience cheered as Romola climbed on to the stage and stood in front of the microphone. I noticed she was wearing pink trousers that I hadn't seen before and a navy-blue top. I gave her a supportive *'Whoop!'*

She held her poem in a trembling hand but looked straight at the audience, her face frowning with concentration.

'Why don't boys wear pink?
Are they scared what boys will think?

Rules like this just stink

Cos girls can wear blue
And go out in trousers too
That's if they want to

Why are girls' toys pink?
Is that what toymakers think?
Are they on the drink?

Why are boys' things blue?
These rules are a load of poo
What can we all do?

We'll decide what's cool
Let's stop being sheep and fools
Kids can change the rules'

Rom dipped her head in a little bow and walked off the stage to rapturous applause. I felt a strange jumble of both pride and envy. Rom's poem was pretty cool. How many more hidden talents did my best friend have? Ingrid patted her on the shoulder and returned to the microphone.

'A fabulous poem that not only stuck to the haiku syllable rules, but *rhymed as well*! That's no easy feat. Well done, Romola! Next up we have Sammy and his poem 'Fever Pitch'. Give it up for Sammy everyone!'

Sammy Green from 6W took to the stage as Rom flopped back into her seat and sighed with relief. I gave her a thumbs up. It was at this point I started to get a flittery fluttery feeling in my belly and my heart lurched into a gallop. Callum squirmed in his seat next to me. I don't think either of us were listening to Sammy's poem about football, but it must've been quite good as the audience gave him a huge cheer.

After Sammy's poem, Ravinda, Javier and Maisie did a poem called 'And Our Survey Said Yeahbut Nobut' that was made up of catchphrases from films and TV shows. Then Richie (wearing fairy wings and deely boppers) and Lucy (sporting a yeti costume and football boots) recited the lyrics to a song called 'Bohemian Rhapsody'. Both acts received big cheers from the audience.

'Our next performer is Fleur,' announced Ingrid, 'with a fabulous little limerick about Brighton and Hove, called 'Rainbow City'. Take it away, Fleur!'

Fleur hopped on to the stage and nervously pushed her

hair behind her ears. Then she stared at the ceiling for a really long time with her mouth half-open.

'Fleur, it's totally fine to read it out if you're having a brain freeze!' whispered Ingrid from the side of the stage.

Fleur jolted and took a folded piece of paper out of her pocket and opened it up.

''Rainbow City',' she announced.

'I live in Brighton-on-Sea
It's a totally rainbow cit-ee
Where to be different is fine
In fact it's divine
There's nowhere else I'd rather be

Hove also seems all right to me
It's next door to Brighton-on-Sea
Some say it's more posh
But that's a load of old tosh
Though its full name is Hove *Actually*'

Everyone clapped as Fleur bowed and hurried off the stage. Ingrid then introduced Noel, whose poem was about climate change, followed by Tomasz, who'd been known as the class brainbox until Callum joined the school.

'And Tomasz will be reciting 'Ace of Spades' by Motörhead – with an added touch of class!' she explained.

I'd been expecting Tomasz to come up with something amazing that he'd written himself, but instead he put on a bow tie and a super-posh voice and recited a song about playing card games. Personally, I didn't think it was anything special, but the adults in the audience obviously loved it because they gave him the loudest round of applause yet. *GrrrrrRRRROWL.*

Another attack of the butterflies took hold of my stomach. I tried taking deep breaths to calm myself down.

'You OK?' whispered Callum.

'Nervous,' I whispered back.

He patted me on the back. 'Me too. Especially in these jeans.'

I was so taken aback by the friendly pat on the back that I pretty much spent the whole of Damon's Shakespeare– Abba lyrics mash-up in a state of shock.

'And now for the penultimate act of the evening,' declared Ingrid. 'Please give a big round of applause for Callum and Clementine and their poem, 'When Things Change'.'

Me and Callum mounted the stage. I cleared my throat

while Callum adjusted the mic. I grinned at Lottie while Dad held up his phone ready to film us. I looked at Lyn, too. She winked at me and nudged Viv who let out a massive squawk. From the middle of the audience, Mel was smiling proudly at Callum.

Callum and I glanced at each other, then he began.

'I didn't like my situation
Things weren't going my way
My parents split up – commiserations
I definitely didn't feel OK.'

[Me]
'I didn't like my situation
Things started changing too quickly
I guess I had a bad reaction
I felt all scratchy and prickly.'

[Callum]
'I felt safe holding on to the past
I thought things would soon turn around
I didn't believe their troubles could last
But I was wrong – we were all future-bound.'

[Me]

'I didn't take to the change very well
I admit my behaviour was bad
I thought things were going to be hell
I felt worried and also quite sad.'

[Callum]

'I wasn't helpful and I wasn't kind
I was angry and wanted everyone to know it
It was all such a jumble inside my mind
I was scared but didn't want to show it.'

[Me]

I was cunning and clever but also quite naughty
I thought I was totally right
Now I'm ashamed that I was so haughty
Apparently, it's known as 'hindsight'.'

[Both of us together]

'We panicked, we fought, we snarked and we meddled
We thought we knew what was best
Now we're doing all we can to back-pedal
But perhaps we should give it a rest.

'When you feel anxious about the future
It's hard to just wait and see
Sometimes the fear's just all inside here
And out there everything's as it should be.'

We bowed to the audience and exited the stage to whoops and cheers. I glanced at Callum's beaming face.

'We did it!' I nudged him.

'We rocked!' He grinned at me.

Ingrid high-fived us both as she headed back to the microphone.

'That was absolutely beautiful, thanks guys! And now for our final act of the evening, please make some noise for Tabitha and her recital of Kate Bush's 'Wuthering Heights'.'

The audience clapped as Tabitha took to the stage. I let out a long, deep breath as my stomach finally started to calm down. Tabitha was giving a pretty good performance until Viv squawked, 'Hasta la vista', bang in the middle of it and made everyone laugh. Luckily, Tabitha saw the funny side and managed to carry on without forgetting the words.

After her performance, the hall began to buzz with murmuring and fidgeting. Ingrid returned to the microphone.

'And now folks, while the judges make their final

decisions, I present to you Miss Lyn Ferno, and her first live performance in nearly *three decades*.'

The audience cheered so loudly it hurt my ears. Clearly my dad wasn't the only Lyn Ferno fan sitting in the school hall. Lyn climbed slowly and carefully on to the stage with Viv sitting on her shoulder. She was dressed in a black jump suit with a tartan belt, and her orange mohawk quivered gently in the draft. I looked at her feet – her roller skates had been replaced by bright red Doc Martens boots.

'Hello, everyone. I'm Lyn and this is Viv. I apologise for the interruption earlier – he's a bit of a chatterbox. Anyway, I'll crack on with it as it wouldn't be fair to keep the kids in suspense about the results any longer than necessary. I thought every single act was brilliant, by the way. So, here's my poem.' She took a piece of paper from her pocket and unfolded it. 'I would tell you the title, but I only wrote it a few hours ago and I haven't got one yet. Here goes:

'Things went pear-shaped, belly up and Pete Tong
Or for those of you that catch my drift
Things fell apart, died and went wrong
Shall I make this a rhyming poem? No, I don't think
I will actually

Rewind a bit to when I was tough, and somewhat
  intimidating
Stirring up trouble was what I enjoyed
Like saying, 'Oi! What you insinuating?'
I was all mouth and no trousers, if the truth be told

But I digress, let's get back to when the sadness
  took hold
I found myself way out of my depth
I was no longer that punk with the attitude so bold
I often cried myself to sleep with a teddy bear
if you must know

And then along came this kid – broke into my house
A head full of poems and worries
Her confidence was gone, she was shy as a mouse
Till I told her I had a wall that was way too
  magnolia for its own good and desperately
  needed some words on it

Her poetry returned – as did her self-belief
My wall became a window to sunshine
This insightful kid helped me deal with my grief

And also pointed out some truths I wasn't quite
   ready for – the bloomin' clever clogs

This poem-loving kid, she taught me a lot
I thought I was the teacher – turns out I'm not
She brought me back to life when I'd started to rot
Thought I was done with friends, but a friend was
   what I got – one that gave me a much-needed
   kick up the cockadoodledoo

'Cockadoddledoo!' squawked Viv.

Which brings me to this celebration of words
   spoken and read
It's a long time since I stood up to say things unsaid
I became a scaredy old goat hiding in the warmth
   of her bed
But then a little bird said, 'Maybe punk really
   is dead?'
And well . . . I couldn't let her get away with being
   right now, could I?'

Lyn looked straight at me and winked. My heart somersaulted

300

with pride. She'd given up her bed-in because of *me*! She called me an 'insightful kid'! I wasn't sure what 'insightful' meant, but I guessed it meant wise. She thought I was *wise*! *Me???* My head was spinning. I remembered the moment I ignored my hammering heart and told her maybe punk *was* dead. *She'd listened to me!* I'd helped her! Perhaps I wasn't such a terrible person after all.

'Thank you for having me.' Lyn gave a polite nod and climbed carefully down from the stage to thunderous applause. I wanted to run over to her and give her a hug, but Ingrid was straight back on the stage waving an envelope.

'Lyn Ferno, everybody!' she cheered. 'Thank you so much, Lyn. And now the moment you've all been waiting for – the decisions are in and Mrs Barraclough is going to come on stage to tell us who the winner is.'

Mrs Barraclough joined Ingrid next to the mic, her shiny brown fringe reflecting the stage lighting.

'Thanks, Ms Partridge. Firstly, a huge thank you to Lyn Ferno, who I've been a dedicated fan of for many, many years. I'm even the proud owner of a signed *Black Eye Suits Ya, Mate* album, would you believe it?' She glanced at Lyn, who was trying to stifle a burp while making her way back to her seat. 'Anyway, next I'd like to thank all the acts for

participating tonight. For having the courage to share their ideas and interpretations with all of us. You entertained us and gave us food for thought. Each act was creative, regardless of whether it was original material or a fresh take on someone else's words. But, of course, there can be only one winner.'

Callum and I stiffened in our seats.

'But before we announce the winner,' she continued, 'we'd like to acknowledge two very close runners-up in Fleur Harris with her 'Rainbow City' poem and Damon Price with his 'Voulez-Vous a Pound of Flesh' poem. Stand up, guys – a big round of applause for these two highly original acts, please.'

Callum and I glanced at each other as the audience clapped. *We were in with a chance of winning!*

'And, before I announce the winner, I'd just like to make one more special mention, as I know this poem was hastily put together by two people who were barely talking to each other earlier this week. It's a testament to their maturity that not only were they able to put their differences to one side, they were able to work together and write a poem that was refreshingly brave and honest. Please give a big round of applause for Callum and Clementine!' Mrs

Barraclough beamed at us and gestured for us to stand up.

Callum sighed, but I nudged him to his feet. 'Come on,' I said.

We stood up together and smiled at the audience (or fake-smiled in Callum's case) while everyone cheered.

'Knew we wouldn't win,' muttered Callum.

'It's not always about winning,' I said, as we sat back down again. 'We're in this to make our parents happy again, remember?'

Callum managed to smile. 'Yeah, suppose so.'

'And the winner is . . .' Mrs Barraclough left an X-Factor-length pause before holding up the book-token-shaped envelope that Ingrid had just handed to her. 'Noel Barratt with 'Earth Needs Help'.'

Everyone whooped and clapped as Noel marched on to the stage to receive his prize and shake Mrs Barraclough's and Ingrid's hands.

'And so, we've reached the end of our show,' said Ingrid, as Mrs Barraclough returned to her seat next to Mr C and Ms Wallace. 'Thank you all so much for coming and supporting this fantastic event. And a special thank you to the legendary Lyn Ferno for stepping in to perform at the very last minute. Mr C will be in touch next week to let you know how much money you helped to raise towards the school library. In the meantime, can we please give Mr C a round of applause for organising this wonderful evening. Good night everyone. *Viva poetry!*'

After showing some seriously loud appreciation for Mr C, people started getting up and gathering their coats. I looked from my dad, across the hall, to Mel. This was the moment.

I turned to Callum. 'Do you think our poem worked?'

He shrugged. 'Guess we're about to find out.'

CHAPTER 26

ONE MINUTE LATER...

AS THE HALL STARTED TO EMPTY, I RAN OVER TO DAD AND LOTTIE WHO WERE CHATTING TO MR C AND INGRID.

'Well done, Clem, you were brilliant!' Ingrid fist-bumped me.

'Super-impressive,' said Mr C, doffing his trilby. 'You should feel very proud of yourself – as should Callum.'

'Clementine! A sterling performance!' cheered Lyn, joining us with Pascal.

Mr C shook Lyn's hand. 'Thank you so much for stepping in – it's an honour to have you here.'

'We're so over you're here,' blurted Dad. 'I mean, we're so moon you're over.'

O.M. Actual G. Embarrassing. Who is this person?

'Third time lucky.' Dad took a deep breath. 'We're so *over the moon* you're here!'

I sighed with relief.

'Well, it's all thanks to Clementine, really,' said Lyn. 'She wanted me to be here and although I was initially reluctant to leave my lair, I realised I couldn't let her down because . . .' Lyn turned to me and took my hand in hers. 'Because A) You asked for my support, and 2) It seems I owe it to you, seeing as you've given me the desire to embrace life again.'

'You helped me, too,' I said. 'I wouldn't have had the courage to enter this competition if it weren't for you.'

'And I wouldn't have performed here tonight – and thoroughly enjoyed myself – if it weren't for you.'

We gave each other a hug.

'Let me take a photo!' said Pascal, ushering us all into a group.

'Wait – we need Callum and Mel, too,' I said.

I looked around and spotted Callum standing with his mum, several rows away. Lottie rushed over to them.

'Like your outfit,' said Ingrid, eyeing up Pascal's tartan suit.

'Why, thank you!' gushed Pascal. 'Although Monsieur C has extraordinarily courageous style for a teacher – I am most impressed!' He nodded towards Mr C's leggings.

'Hi, everyone,' said Mel awkwardly, as Lottie herded her and Callum towards us.

'Hi,' said Dad, just as awkwardly. 'Great performance, Callum!'

'OK, everybody please gather together and say 'fromage',' said Pascal.

We all posed for the camera.

'WAIT!' I called out. Pascal lowered his phone. 'STAND AND DELIVER!' I patted my shoulder and Viv flew from Lyn to me, landing on my wrist. I put my free arm around Callum's shoulder. 'OK, ready!'

'*Fromage!*' we all cheered.

'*C'est bon!*' Pascal gave us the thumbs up.

'Clementine, you and Callum were great,' said Mel. 'What an amazing poem. It was really heart-warming.'

'Thank you,' I said. 'I also wanted to say sorry about my behaviour before. I wasn't very nice to you.'

Mel smiled. 'Thank you. Let's say no more about it.' She gave me a friendly squeeze on the shoulder and turned to Mr C. 'Thanks for lending Callum your jeans, Mr C. Would it be OK if we returned them freshly washed on Monday?'

'Of course,' said Mr C. 'They suit him.'

Callum gave a sheepish grin.

'Thank you – you're a lifesaver.' Mel turned to Dad and smiled. 'Well, we'd best be off – got to pop to the Co-op for a few groceries before we head home. Good to see you, Ray. Bye everyone, take care.'

'See you,' said Dad, as Mel and Callum headed out of the hall.

Was that it? Couldn't they at least say a bit more than just 'Hi' and 'Bye'? Lottie and I exchanged disappointed glances. What could we do, though? Had Operation Good Romance reached a dead end already?

'We'd better get on with the tidying up, hadn't we, Mr C?' said Ingrid.

'Guess so,' said Mr C. 'Bye everyone, thanks for coming.'

'I've got a little surprise in store,' announced Lyn as Mr C and Ingrid left us to go and stack up the chairs.

Dad, Lottie and I leant in closer.

'To celebrate the end of my bed-in and Clementine Florentine's first live poetry performance, I've booked a table at a little milkshake bar that Pascal tells me is *très bon*. Would you do me the honour of joining me? It's my treat.'

Dad looked at me and Lottie. 'Sounds good to me – what d'you reckon, kids?'

'Do they do banana milkshakes?' asked Lottie.

'I believe they do every flavour of milkshake you could ever think of, including my personal favourite, *salted caramel*!' grinned Pascal.

Lottie's eyes lit up.

'Is it far?' asked Dad. 'Only, we walked here.'

'Well, I've taken the liberty of hiring a car,' explained Lyn. 'Thought it might be fun to arrive in style – *in true vintage punk style*, that is. Follow me, everyone. Pascal, you did make sure they were delivering the car to the school and not our home address, didn't you?'

Pascal rolled his eyes. '*Oui*, your majesty, of course I did!'

We trooped out of the hall, through the main doors, through the school gates and on to the pavement where we ground to an abrupt halt, our eyes on stalks.

'Gordon Bennett!' squawked Viv on my shoulder.

'O.M. ACTUAL G!' I squealed.

'NO WAY!' shouted Lottie, jumping up and down.

'That's . . . um . . . that's . . .' Dad stammered, lost for words.

'PASCAL!' yelled Lyn. 'WHAT IN THE NAME OF RAT SCABIES IS THAT?'

Parked right outside the school gates, and taking up at least five parking spaces, was a mahoosively long, bright pink car that looked more like a single-decker bus.

'They didn't have any vintage Jags,' shrugged Pascal. 'So I thought maybe a stretch Hummer Limo would be fun! It's got disco lights and glitter balls inside – what's not to like?'

'It's a *monstrosity*,' gasped Lyn.

'It's amaaaaaaazing!' I swooned, itching to climb in.

'DOES IT HAVE A SWIMMING POOL?' screamed Lottie.

'No, I'm afraid not. But it has a minibar full of fizzy drinks.' Pascal winked at us. 'I think the Hummer is a winner, *Madame* Ferno!'

Dad laughed. 'Well, the kids love it, so I'm game if you are.'

Lyn threw up her arms in defeat. 'OK, fine. I'm outnumbered.'

A chauffeur stepped out of the driver's seat door and greeted us. 'Whenever you're ready, sirs, madams.' He opened the passenger side door and stood aside while Lottie dived in, buzzing with excitement, followed by Pascal.

'Can Rom come, too?' I asked, spotting Rom and her parents coming out of the school gates. 'And her mum and dad?'

'The more, the merrier,' smiled Lyn. 'It's about time I got to know some of my neighbours.'

I waved Rom over and pointed to the Limo. 'Giulia and Ranvir, would you like to join us in Lyn's Limo?'

'It's not *my* Limo – God forbid!' Lyn explained as they walked over to us. 'I was hoping to hire a Jaguar, but it appears this was all they had left.'

Lyn introduced herself to Rom's parents and they shook hands.

'Come on, guys,' said Dad. 'We're going for milkshakes!'

'That's very kind, but are you sure there's enough room for all of us in there?' asked Giulia.

'Only one way to find out!' squealed Rom, giving me a hug and diving in before her parents could say no.

Suddenly 'Le Freak' boomed out of the Limo's sound system at top volume.

'TUUUUNE!' Ranvir cheered. 'Count us in!' He climbed in after Rom, followed by Giulia.

Lyn nudged me. 'Isn't that Callum and his mum over there?'

Me and Dad turned round. Callum and Mel were walking towards us with a bag of groceries, their eyes fixed on the pink Limo.

'Care to join us?' asked Lyn, as they drew nearer. 'The party's just getting started and there's still heaps of room.'

'That's very kind, but we need to get home,' said Mel, lifting up her bag of groceries.

Callum turned to his mum. 'Come on, Mum! There might be a swimming pool inside!'

Lyn chuckled. 'Not sure about a swimming pool but, as you can hear, there is *definitely* a disco.'

'And glitter balls, a minibar, disco lights,' said Dad. 'It would be a shame not to use up all that luxury pink seating.'

'Please come, Mel,' I said. 'We're going for milkshakes.'

Mel bit her lip.

'I would really love it if you and Callum could join us,' Dad gave Mel his best smoulder. Her lips twitched into a smile.

If Dad could smoulder, then so could I. I dug deep within my soul for the supernatural power I was *certain* I possessed.

'It won't be the same without you,' I said, unleashing my super-shamazing aura and letting it surround her like the aroma of a freshly opened packet of cheese Doritos.

Mel inhaled and smiled.

Callum tugged at her arm. *'Please?'*

'Go on, then,' she said. 'Thanks. We'd love to.'

YES! I HAD THE POWER!

'Splendid!' Lyn clapped her hands excitedly. 'All aboard – Brighton's calling!'

Dad stepped aside to let Mel, Callum and Lyn climb into the Limo. I was just about to follow them when Dad put his hand on my shoulder.

'I'm proud of you, Clem-cakes.'

I beamed. 'Proud of you, too, Dad.'

'Bing bong!' chirped Viv from my shoulder.

'Oh, and Clem?'

'Yes, Dad?'

'Keep that pooing parrot away from me or there'll be trouble.'

RUDE!

Dear reader,

Thank you so much for reading this book – I hope it lifted your spirits. If you want to know what inspired me to write this story, read on!

Clementine is fairly similar to a girl I used to know: *Me*. In year 6, I had a super-cool teacher who I was desperate to impress, but due to my tendency to show off, I often achieved the exact opposite. Like Clementine, I once hurled mashed potato across the canteen at my nemesis Phil Jenkins* – not my smartest move. (I was Simpkinned immediately). A few years later in Year 10 (and old enough to know better), I stuck chewing gum under a desk, which later ruined Cheryl Evans's* skirt. I blatantly denied I had anything to do with it until the teacher pointed out it could only have been me. So that year, too, I sabotaged my chances of becoming a star pupil.

But when it came to writing, I was in my element. I loved nothing more than to write poems, stories and plays. When I needed to get something off my chest, I would grab my diary and ramble on for pages – often including passionate or plain silly poems. Writing a diary helped me through good times and bad – and still does to this day.

Like Clementine, there were times when I felt pretty pleased with myself, and times when I felt mortifying levels of shame. Clementine learns (as I'm learning, much later in life) that situations aren't always as black or white as they first seem. And nor are people. She learns that everyone makes mistakes – not least herself – and no matter how despairing you might feel, the moment and the feeling eventually pass. We are all a work-in-progress and every day is a clean, new page.

As the poet Rainer Maria Rilke said over 100 years ago in his poem, Go to the Limits of Your Longing: 'Just keep going. No feeling is final.'

Warmest wishes,
Tasha Harrison

*Not their real names!

ACKNOWLEDGEMENTS

I would like to thank . . .

Melissa Welliver, Marisa Noelle, Lindsay Sharman, Sharon Hopwood, Caitlin Price-Stephens, Ralph Browning, Lydia Massiah, Julie Marnie Leigh & Renee McAlpine: I'm lucky to have such a lovely bunch of Curtis Brown Creative writing comrades to cheer each other on through the highs and lows of this writing life!

Caroline Ambrose at Bath Children's Novel Awards: Thank you for being such a champion of unpublished authors. Making it to the shortlist of BNAKids in 2017 with my previous manuscript, and the longlist in 2018 with Clementine, were two invaluable boosts to my then flagging confidence. I'm so grateful to all the junior judges who gave both novels the thumbs up.

Thanks also to **the #WriteMentor community and Jedi-in-Chief, Stuart White:** I'm so glad to be a part of this friendly and supportive community that's enabled me to connect with so many other lovely writers from all stages of the writing journey.

Alison Porges, Sharon Sutherland and Nichole Fox: Thank you for sharing your utterly gross and hilarious animal anecdotes, and for allowing me to adapt and use them in Clementine. Where there's muck, there's laughs!

Sam Westcott: Thank you for allowing me to feature the real Eddie Two-Balls who, it should be noted, is way better behaved than his fictional namesake! (And yes, it's true he can fit three tennis balls in his mouth).

Jen Jahn and Dorothy Koomson: Thank you both for all your writerly and readerly support over the years.

Julia Faiers, Lola & Betsy W, Jenny Bate, Zac & Tilly H: Thank you for reading various drafts of one novel or another over the years and for giving me encouraging feedback and hope.

Lottie H: Thank you for letting me borrow your name and one of your many talents!

My amazing agent Lauren Gardner at Bell Lomax Moreton: Thank you for all your support, encouragement and spot-on advice, the greatest of which is pinned to my wall: 'LET RIP!' (Which is open to interpretation, but *I* know what you mean).

Hazel Holmes, Kathy Webb, Becky Chilcott, Kieran Baker: A huuuge thank you to the talented, expert and super-supportive team at UCLan Publishing who have worked so hard to bring this book to life. Thank you for believing in me and Clementine. And thank you to the super-talented **Mya Mitchell** for the brilliant illustrations.

The late Sue Townsend: For writing so many funny, warm-hearted novels that inspired my own writing. Punk legend Lyn Ferno is 100% fictional, but her bed-in was inspired by the novel *The Woman Who Went To Bed For A Year*.

Mum & Dad: Thank you for always encouraging my writing endeavours. PS: Before you go telling your friends your daughter is now an 'accomplished author', you should know this book has the word fart in it. More than once.

My amazing daughters: Thanks for being my trusty preliminary editors, and for giving me such helpful feedback. Who would have known that your once incessant demands for on-the-spot made-up bedtime stories would lead me to writing children's fiction?

Mr H: Thank you for being my rock and my champion, supporting my writing journey non-stop for over 20 years. When my self-belief was at its lowest, you persuaded me to keep going. You've inspired me, encouraged me and given me some of my best lines. Love you big time.